Quantum

events

George Opacic

Quantum Events

Author: George Opacic

Publisher: Rutherford Press

For information, contact:

Rutherford Press,
PO Box 648
Qualicum Beach, BC, Canada V9K 1A0
info@rutherfordpress.ca

https://rutherfordpress.ca

ISBN (book) # 978-1-988739-25-0
ISBN (ebook) # 978-1-988739-26-7

As I understand it, "variety is the spice of life". These stories are sprinkled with life's spices and have emerged from the oven in a variety of formats and genres. I hope you enjoy them as much as I did in seeing them come to fruition.

Acknowledgments

The very patient assistance of my wife is gratefully acknowledged. Without Darlene's kind presence, to read, comment on, and perform the myriad administrative tasks involved in writing and publishing, I would have been lost. Two long-standing friends deserve special mention. James Harrold has been a scrupulous editor of several of these works, as well as a willing foil in discussions philosophical. If a typo has slipped past, it is likely to have come from rewrites which he did not see.

Ben Nuttall-Smith, whose works grace the portfolio offered by Rutherford Press, and whose delightful paintings brighten our house, has been a friend, co-conspirator and confidant. Ben's wise commentary on my random walk through literature has always been welcome.

Numerous writers, poets and organizers within the literary community of British Columbia, particularly in the Federation of BC Writers, should be mentioned. Alas, my infamously poor memory for names will allow me to place only these few here (I do apologize profusely to those with whom I had hours of conversation, but failed to remember their names): Sheilagh Simpson, Barbara Botham, Ben Nuttall-Smith, Margo Lamont, Loreena Lee, Adam Fortunate Eagle, Norbi Rittinghaus, Rachel McMillen...

CONTENTS

Pretending To Be Human — 1

The Universe Is Shrinking — 4

The Land is Life — 11

The Clinker — 17

Is God Dead? — 25

Corporate M & A — 49

Living in a Pingo — 55

Skytrain Desultory — 63

Do They Walk Among Us? — 68

Visitor — 73

Unbonding — 84

The Future of the Future — 98

Love Is War — 101

Bus Delivery — 117

Squids and Free Will — 128

Searching For Fate 140

The Cub 161

Moebius Slip 167

BOXES 215

If you were a neandertal pretending to
be human, what would you see around
you?
If your people had walked with ancient
dwellers on this land, how would you
feel about the present humans who so
vainly assert rampant *ownership?*
Take my hand as I guide you through the
mind of another type of human.
It may sound like being in a coma
dreaming.

PRETENDING TO BE HUMAN

by a neoandertal

(imagine Glenn Gould playing Bach's toccata BWV 910)

Time lies still-borne in void-black free space...
except for that unbearably tiny singularity.

Then, in a fantastic turbulence of uncontainable light,
Fat colourful letters chase amorphous strings which all fade into
        WORDS
              each a translucent bag of meaning
                   containing words
                      within words
But they careen off madly against grey numbers and greekletter-thingies,
    like a tetraplex of billiard balls each with its own spectrum
    of stickiness and deference and smile and fear and curiosity,
    or lifeless thunk...
Empty black stretches to eternity...except for us quantum billiard balls.
    Then

Dots resolve uncertainty
into a shimmering haze of moisture
clinging against a coarse slope of awareness
veiling your plodding climb past totems of perception

where
      the signposts dissolve
          into the future,
              speeding beyond the arrow of time
                  enticing its point into slow dissolution.

A slippery bell curve awaits
　　　　trapping the unwary down its slopes to the foothills,
　　　　　　　lower, to the endless desert of 5 standard deviations.
Everywhere,
a pregnant feathery sphere, found within a sphere, in a sphere...
Similarity, constant similarity boring to the depths of
　　　　　　　　　　endless mirrors of almost itself
　　　　At each scale, with a trifling dust speck in its works,
　　　　　　　the similarity morphs into a marvelous
　　　　　　　　　wriggling mass of

Dancing fractalating carbons that join with oxygen and friends
　　　　Folding into a mirror, a helix, a force

Life　　a w a k e n s .

A dark fuzziness grows in my amygdala
Pulling the hairs on my scalp from within.
A stark fuzziness takes my mind from without,
Where white is black and she is he and life is,
Life is only marginally more tempered than not-life.

Seeing is bedeviling.
When is Reality now?
Is it only real after it is masticated into memory?
My eyes are not your eyes, so whose eyes truly see?

Should I jump into the trembling abyss of tomorrow,
Armed with knowing only that I know little?
Should I smile at this stranger,
Lead with angst on my open sleeve,
As she gazes with doubt below my eyes
At my heart of fearful smiles?
To jump? Or to sleep forever
　　　　in the safe gauze of youthful certainty.
Until she speaks, she is a character in my mind's play.

A beginning for her starts with an event.
Time for him is relative,
          part of the whole,
                    pulled out by a pointing finger,
                         to be analyzed.

Entangled, the probabilistic string between them sings a tense inframelody.
    He cries, she flinches, feeling a cold breath on her fifth dimension.

"In the news today", says the radio,
"Roseanne fights and beats Super Mario;
The pope has an audience with Vincent Rosario;
A new wave of riots in a latin barrio;
Toddler sues doctor to provide her a penis;
Assad elected Chair of UN Civil Rights Office;
Guards shoot teacher stringing rainbow display;
And inclement weather claims new victims, today."

Disentangling, the probabilistic string between them flops discordantly.
He cringes in pain.
She brushes her hair,
          hopping randomly between colourful dimensions,
                    wondering why there is a loose knot
                              and who wanted it tied, anyway.

The Nine Quanta of Our Hololife
Dreaming in a coma
Reaming in a comad
Eaming in a comadr
Aming in a comadre
Ming in a comadrea
Ing in a comadream
Ng in a comadreami
G in a comadreamin
In a comadreaming.

THE UNIVERSE IS SHRINKING

It's 4:18.

"I went on a trip yesterday."

"Where did you go?"

Her smile is a bit mischievous. Her dentures gleam.

"Oh, we went a long way. Dorothy and I were taken to that park beside the waterfall – Niagara Falls."

"Niagara Falls!?"

And then he calms down.

"Mom, did you go on the trip yesterday?"

"Well, yes. No. The day before…" She looks out the window. "I'm not sure, now that you asked…"

He notices movement in the backyard. A dark grey cat is lounging against the sun-warmed garden shed on the far side of a manicured lawn. He looks to his mother.

"Is that cat always there, mom?"

"Cat? What cat?…"

He sits back in his chair.

It's 4:31.

"Is there a cat out there? Reach me my glasses, will you, son?…"

She squints at the picture window.

"That's why the birds don't visit anymore…"

He reaches for her glasses and places them on her lap. Then he picks up the tv remote, flicking on a nature show.

"Damn cats."

"Maybe that's why there's no rabbits in the yard, either, eh, mom?"

She nods.

It's 4:45.

"Mom. Can I help you down to the dining room?"

"What?"

"Would you like to go on a trip with me down to the dining room?"

"Oh can we?... That would be great fun."

She pulls her sweater down her hips then rocks a bit to get up. She stops.

"Oh, son. Can you find my slippers? I'm not sure where I left them."

Seeing them just under the bed next to her feet, he pulls them out and helps her slip them on.

"Son, can you please take a look, sometime, in the shoe stores, for a nice pair of shoes? These slippers are very good, but they're starting to feel funny inside... Take a look at them, will you?"

He pulls off the old slippers. His mother's feet are ninety-one years old, with dark blotches from her swollen ankles up to her calves. Her feet are flat and scrunched, looking like they've been contained tightly for, well, ninety years. They are almost as wide as they are long.

Nobody makes shoes to fit her. He's tried and tried.

Ten years ago, when his mother was still quite active, they had gone to a shoe store. The pair that sort-of fit were soon put in the closet because they were too slippery and heavy. They are still there. The slippers they found then are what she is now wearing. They don't make the right kind of slippers anymore – some are too sticky on the floor, or too slippery, or the metal on them somewhere tingles her nerves. Several new pairs are in the closet with the shoes.

"You're right, mom. The lining is rumpled a bit. I'll just cut the lumps out… Your scissors still in the drawer?"

"If somebody hasn't taken them. Try that drawer… Or maybe the…"

"Here they are. Just be a minute."

He turns off the television as he sits down to work on the slippers.

It's 4:58.

He snips the frayed lining from both slippers, then smooths down the insides.

"Here, let me put them back on. Let's see if that's better."

Her old socks, partly rolled off her feet, cover the swollen and discoloured legs. Looking at them, his gut shivers deeply.

As he gently pulls the socks on, being sure not to make them too tight, he makes a note to try to set a few dollars aside to buy her some new socks, at least. This place is taking every penny he has. He puts her slippers over the socks.

"There. Now let me help you up, mom."

"Ok. Where're we going, son?"

"For a walk down to the dining room. It'll be supper time soon... Then I'm going to have to get on the road. Have'ta take a load to Cincinnati."

"You're going already, son?"

"Yes, mom. Gotta pay the bills... But first we'll go on a trip to the dining room."

"Oh son, I haven't given you anything to eat or drink. There's some cookies in one of the drawers – if they haven't taken them. The girls are very nice, but as soon as I leave the room, they go through all the drawers and take the cookies and fruit and who knows what else..."

"Yes mom. They said they have to, to keep down the mice and things."

"Oh."

He reaches for her walker. "Here's your machine. Is it working alright, now?"

"Yes. The tune-up helped… It's just…"

She settles her arms along the handles.

"These handles are really uncomfortable. And when my hands touch the metal, the electricity goes right into my arms."

"Well, I've been looking for something that would work better. They don't seem to have the right parts. I'll keep looking, mom…"

A long shuffle gets them to the dining room. It is right at the exit. He steers her gently toward the drinks table.

It's 5:19.

"Mom, would you like a juice, now, or a banana?"

She looks around the dining room.

"Oh, no thanks, son. They've nearly finished setting up for… Is this breakfast?"

"It's supper time. The board says that you'll be having ham with mashed potatoes and peas. Sounds good, doesn't it?" He nods encouragingly.

A server hustles from the kitchen with the last of the plates and cutlery.

"I'll sit over there at my table. That's my table – just Dorothy and me, now. Emile's gone. Dorothy doesn't want to leave. One of the girls wanted to move her to the other side but she said, NO, I'm not leaving Eva! She helps me, she said." She smiles and nods with purpose.

They get to the table.

"I help her take the right pills. Heh heh. She forgets things easily. But she doesn't want to leave."

She coughs once, then fights down another one.

He forces himself to gaze into her eyes as she speaks to him. It is hard. He sees the darkness creeping in again. When she had pneumonia last month he thought the light had gone out then. His mother had fought back, holding his hand tightly as he stayed with her for the week. The residence guest room was expensive, but...

"Mom. Give me a kiss. I'm going to have to go now."

She gives her son a big kiss.

"Bye, son. Why don't you take a snack with you?"

"That's alright. I'll be stopping for supper soon... Well, maybe I'll just have a cookie and some juice."

At the snack table he wraps up the cookie in a serviette, then puts it in a pocket. Pouring some orange juice into a glass, he glugs it down, thinking that it will save him a bit of money at supper down the road. If he stops.

Ready, he gives his mother a wave.

"Now you take it easy driving that big truck of yours," she says lightly.

"Bye mom. See you next week."

A hidden cough behind her hand, then a weak "Bye" sends him on his way.

As he leaves, he smiles at the stone fountain outside the entrance that she calls Niagara Falls. The park benches and umbrellaed tables are occupied by people taking in the afternoon sun. Some of them are rising for the 5:30 meal.

His rig is parked on the road half a block down.

It's 5:27.

He wipes his nose and eyes, then pats the cookie in his pocket.

THE LAND IS LIFE

Kugaaruk, Nunavut

Spring

On the edge of the northern town, nestled among rocks and light brown sand, a peeling pre-fab's door creaks to let out an older Inuk hunter. Dressed in an open seal-skin coat and with its parka flopping on his back, he strides smoothly past his twenty-two year old son. The hunter is preparing his wooden sled for a last excursion on the spring ice.

A tin can of water he carries is carefully held inside the flap of his coat against the cold. The hunter's son sits sideways on a yellow snowmobile. He shakes his head at his father.

The light wooden and bone sled is tightly strapped together with leather strips. It is lying runners up. The old hunter pulls a folded cloth from an inside pocket and shakes it free of lint. The cold wind carries the lint away from the sled.

The sharp blue sky has a sun in it, though there is no heat in its rays. Downslope from his little home on the edge of the community, a rocky shore can be seen running into a choppy Pelly Bay. The last of this season's growler ice floes still sway on the ocean between Kugaaruk and rocky islands that are an easy boat ride away. In the distance, the sea is covered in old ice that has heaved everywhere into a treacherous landscape.

The son is zipped tightly into a bright green nylon coat whose artificial fur hood tries to keep his face warm. New yellow leather boots and dark green insulated nylon pants all seem to make little rubbing noises even as he sits there in the frigid spring air. He wipes his nose ineffectually with a nylon sleeve.

"Dad, I don't know why you refuse to get modern. I can help you to screw on the plastic strips to those runners. It'll make you go easier - the dogs won't have to work so hard. I don't know why you want to keep dogs, anyway. Get with the times, dad."

Carrying on with long established motions, the hunter dips the cloth into his tin can of water. He carefully rubs the wet cloth along a runner, starting from the front. Keeping the application of water smooth and thin, it freezes quickly onto the runner. Each application is merged with the next one so that the surface stays smooth. His work is hypnotic to the young man. As the first coat is finished, the hunter goes back to do it again.

Rousing from his trance, the son sniffs and shakes his head, "All this time you waste…"

"My son, ice is more slippery than your plastic. And when that southern material chips or breaks on a rock, can you smooth it down, two days away, with the weight of a seal, in a blizzard? No. My iced runners are strong. If they chip, when I stop for tea I will make more water and smooth my runners again. Wherever I am."

He looks pointedly at his son's scratched up snowmobile skis. "And when I take such care with my qamutik and my other important tools, I treat them with respect."

The young man squirms in his seat. A creak of the door alerts him to his mother emerging from the house. She is dressed in her bright clothes. Closing the door securely, she speaks to both her husband and her son. "I'm going to the church for a while. I don't want you two arguing while I'm away. Mikey? OK?"

Her son nods, head down, "Yes mom."

As she disappears down the lane the old hunter mumbles, "Bingo." He turns back to exchange a grin with his son.

Hesitating to bring up a sore point, the hunter starts quietly, "That new friend of yours, Mikey – we welcomed him to our place and fed him our best food. He spat it out. He gave you, not me, a bag that was full of many new things from the south. The far-seeing glasses…"

"Binoculars, dad."

"…can be very useful on a trek." He nods. "What is that other envelope and secret bag you are holding for him?"

Eyes down, "Nothing, dad. Just something to pass on to somebody on the next airplane. He gave me that contract. I will work for him." He beams, sitting up straight. "And he gave me a secret mission…" then trails off, remembering the word "secret".

Still holding the can of water under his coat the hunter shakes his head slowly, knowing that his son is not going down a path that will benefit him. "It is good to learn the ways of qallunaat, the southern people. Learn what they know and what they value. They have much to offer you. But you must also learn who you are and what the land will do to you. It may be that you will not need to hunt seals for your food. Your new friend, and the store," he nods in the direction of the prominent new two-storey building in the middle of Kugaaruk, "they bring many tasty things. Some of it is food, and some of it may satisfy your tummy. But you must know that it is southern food, made for southern tummies that do not fuel you against this Arctic cold. Like those boots that you gave so many hides for. The southern animal of their hide…"

"They call it moose, dad." He kicks at a chunk of sand and snow that is still frozen solid.

"Moose – has not walked on the tundra. Its hide will not protect you when you walk on the tundra. Seal or caribou is the only hide for kamiit that can keep you warm when the sun goes down."

He applies more thin layers of water to the runner.

"My son, the words of the southern people carry many meanings. We have not walked on their land and they have only winged their way over ours. Some of their words carry great danger. It is not the same danger that we might see on the ice. The danger in their words, that we think must be innocent, comes from a land that has accepted violence over pieces of paper. I did not see paper until I was your age. Now paper rules everything, even here on our land. They do not know our land and you do not know their land. Southern people think that words on paper are the only thing that is important.

"I will tell you the truth that you must remember. The man who does not learn to understand and respect the land will too soon become part of it."

He sees no reaction from his son. "If that does not impress you, my son, I must add one more thing I have learned. The worst thing that can happen to you is if the land rejects your contribution to its life-force."

THE CLINKER

A short screen play

EXT. MONTREAL STREET – 1920S, SUMMER EVENING

A young lad, dressed in a checkered suit that needs cleaning, walks awkwardly down the middle of a granite bordered sidewalk. His wide eyes move to check doorways while his head stays straight ahead. A cloth bag in each hand weighs him down more than the size warrants. The distinctive clinking of filled bottles sounds out at each step.

To young JOHN CLARK, the bottles are a clanging of gongs aiming the pointing finger of God directly at his illicit burden.

A flashing lamp in a window brings his eyes up from the fixed downward stare. Shaking off some of his fear, he calls up a reserve of courage, pushing on with a more determined step.

He mumbles encouragement to himself.

                         JOHN CLARK
              After all, if the
              cops are being paid

> off, they should
> make sure nothing
> goes wrong with the
> delivery of this
> cargo. Right?

He nods in agreement with himself.

The Gazette building finally, and thankfully, appears before him. A solemn doorman lets the young fellow in without a word, as if they are both performing part of a sacred ceremony. Over marbled floors to the wrought iron grill of the elevator, trimmed in brass, the acolyte carries his two cloth bags.

The elevator operator, RICHARD, lets him in to his glittering brass cubicle.

RICHARD

> Back safely, lad?

John nods absently while Richard closes the door and starts the elevator moving up.

RICHARD

> What's your name,
> son?

JOHN

> John, sir. John
> Clark.

He brushes a runny nose with a shoulder,
still holding a bag in each hand, and looks
at the operator.

                    JOHN

     And yours?

                  RICHARD

     Richard. Just call me
     Richard.

The uniform on Richard's chest swells out a
bit, then releases with a sigh, as he looks
at the eager young copy boy.

                  RICHARD

     Got your orders
     correct, John?

A tentative nod in answer.

                  RICHARD

     Better make damn
     sure. Did you see
     Flaherty cross off
     some names on the
     list?

A look of sudden terror flashes over John's
face.

                    JOHN
          Cross off names? But,
          but they said to come
          back with exactly the
          right number of
          bottles or they'd
          skin me alive!

The elevator cage becomes a trap to John's
frantic eyes.

                  RICHARD
          Take it easy, take it
          easy, young fellow.

Richard slows the elevator down and stops
it between floors.

                  RICHARD
          Listen, you don't
          understand. This is
          what happens.

Richard holds one hand on the lever that
keeps them half a floor from the reporters'
desks, while his other hand scribes
soothing arcs.

                  RICHARD
          You got everybody's
          liquor order written
          down, right?

An anxious nod.

> **RICHARD**
>> Right. Mr. O'Sullivan
>> gave you specific
>> directions - and the
>> secret knock - right?

A wide-eyed nod.

> **RICHARD**
>> I've done this, too,
>> ah, John.
>>
>> (he smiles at the old memories)
>> So, when you got
>> upstairs, what
>> happened?

Eager to find his way out of his difficult
situation, John speaks freely.

> **JOHN**
>> Well, I couldn't
>> believe it! The whole
>> hallway is stacked to
>> the ceiling with more
>> name brands than I
>> knew existed! And,
>> and Mr. Flaherty just
>> looks at the list and
>> checks off the orders

> and puts bottle after
> bottle in these bags,
> and...

Richard holds up his hand.

> **RICHARD**
> Ok. Now, as Flaherty
> went down the list,
> didn't he put a cross
> beside any name?

John nearly cracks a bottle as he quickly
lowers the bags to the floor to reach into
a pocket for the list. Sure enough, two
names have *X*es beside them. John hastily
crosses himself.

> **JOHN**
> Oh jesus-mother-of-
> god! Mr. Leary! And
> he was the one who
> said he'd skin me
> alive if I didn't
> come back with his
> bottle!

John slumps against the elevator as he
hands the list to Richard.

> **RICHARD**
> Lad, listen.

> (Richard smiles broadly)
>> Mr. Leary ain't going to skin nobody. What this means is that he hasn't paid Flaherty for the last two bottles. If you don't pay, you don't get. He's cut off until Flaherty's been satisfied.

Pulling the lever, Richard starts the elevator moving up again.

RICHARD

>> Don't get into a sweat, John. You just go and take the bottles to their owners. When you come to Mr. Leary and Mr...

> (he glances at the list)
>> and Mr. Gottlieb, you just show them their Xes.

He pulls the doors open. As John picks up
the two bags, Richard stuffs the list back
into John's shirt pocket.

RICHARD

Get on with you, now.

On shaky legs, John walks into the noisy,
smoke-filled reporters' room.

JOHN

This is not what I
had in mind when I
decided to become a
reporter.

IS GOD DEAD?

As yet unknown to each other, two environmental activists, Simion McHugh and Andrei Orlov, are separately sipping their coffees at the back of a coffee shop located on the pier at Canada Place. They are, respectively, from Vancouver and Vladivostok.

With his Russian sensibilities, Andrei is not used to the "different" flavour of an extra large, even with lots of honey and cream. Simion, taller than Andrei, has an incongruously small cup in his long-fingered hands. He wears a subtle stealth-grin as he follows the live theatre in the coffee shop while at the same time scanning selected news feeds on his phablet.

Blond-haired Andrei swipes a curly lock from his eye and slowly checks out the local women. His newly purchased casual clothes sit rather awkwardly on his muscular frame. Compared to the others all multitasking in some way, Andrei seems to be in a slower time-warp. To the recently arrived Russian, the environment is both conceptually familiar and disturbingly foreign. His eyes are drawn hither and yon by each person's isolated entrapment in their electronic device; the scary noise of the capuchilatte machine; the brazen clothing of the young women; the overwhelming number of Asian tourists walking by outside… And everybody in some blurred, quicker dimension.

An older man in a suit enters the coffee shop, trying overly hard to be unobtrusive, so he fails miserably. Andrei gives him a quick, low-key wave.

Director Paluntov is the epitome of awkward in this milieu, with his white, blue and red striped tie, white shirt, dark suit, brown shoes, oversized black briefcase, and furtive glances. Seeing Andrei at a back table, he places a severe finger on his mouth toward Andrei, who immediately puts his head down to stare at the cooling coffee. Paluntov pauses, then goes over to sit at the table beside Andrei, placing his briefcase between them. As he sits down, he whispers with a strong Russian accent, "Is rock."

He looks studiously at the clock on his cellphone, waits thirty seconds, then gets up to leave, sans suitcase.

The manager behind the counter rolls his eyes, thinking, *"Talk about over-acting. I hope they're still practicing. Wonder what film they're doing?"* A cursory scan doesn't reveal any cameras taking a long shot into the coffee shop so he goes back to business. Even so, he angles one of his signs strategically on the top counter.

Simion and Andrei are at an international environmental conference being held in Canada Place. They had been chosen as two of twenty lucky people who had applied to a special program to remediate certain sites around the Arctic.

Andrei had jumped at the chance to go to the Arctic, first submitting his CV and other qualifications in Russian cyrillic, without fully reading the application requirements. He then had to rewrite everything by labouriously translating it into English. When he received his final submission form, signifying that he'd essentially been accepted, he and his girlfriend, Elena, got thoroughly pissed. Actually, she did. Andrei was always in control.

His questioning mind turned to thinking why his girlfriend would be so happy to have him leave for so long.

The phone call saying that official word will come of Andrei's approval, also said that his visa and Russian government approval papers were to be delivered personally by two suits from the Oceanographic Institute in Vladivostok. This personal delivery was most unusual, causing Andrei considerable worry in the three hours between receiving the phone call from a secretary and the time of the meeting. He was told curtly that he was to prepare for a brief meeting at his apartment with Director Paluntov of the Oceanographic Institute, and Juri Gherov, an "Operations Advisor".

Andrei had previously met the older gentleman, Director Paluntov, when Paluntov had been a seminar panel member at a university meeting of "alternative thinkers" a few years ago.

At the time, Andrei had been persuaded by a fellow ex-soldier to join a group of "true patriots" to go with a group to the meeting in a dacha, to heckle the *anti-government academics*, as they were called. Andrei had understood the meeting was to be run by dissidents and funded by a multibillionaire political critic, Mikhail Khodorkovsky.

Andrei had made the mistake of listening to what was said. Engaged in the reasonable arguments despite himself, he'd separated from the hecklers to attend and participate in small-group discussions.

Near the close of the official part of the meeting, Andrei spoke with Paluntov. After polite back-and-forth,

Andrei was asked to follow the older gentleman onto a quiet upstairs patio. It had a concrete balustrade, overlooking a countryside of meadows and forests behind the dacha where the meeting was being held. Inside, Paluntov was carrying his jacket, but he had slipped it back on as they strolled onto the tiled patio. Andrei drank in the late day summer smells of recently trimmed grass and fertile soil wafting in a warm breeze.

Leaning on the white concrete balustrade, staring at the soothing vista of nearby green and yellow meadows lined with mature trees, Paluntov confirmed to a questioning Andrei that he was indeed a staunch Russian patriot, as was Khodorkovsky. However, he was not willing to be deluded by false references to patriotism as a way of blindly towing somebody's party line. He was open to new ideas, he said. For instance, embracing new Western business ideas like quick evidence-based decision-making, despite his years of apparatchik training.

"If it was the situation that I knew everything the day I was born, young man, my first independent action should have been to kill myself. There would have been no reason to carry on. Life is only bearable when it includes learning experiences, punctuated, as it inevitably will be, with the spice of harsh lessons that come out of mistakes and reversals. We must persevere, open our eyes, then open our minds to the new things that may be continually learned and applied, and move forward with the benefit of that knowledge. What good is life without that?"

Andrei had admitted to confusion. "Director, I can tell you my experiences have been, what you say, harsh. I was in the 108th in Afghanistan. That withdrawal was… ugly." He closed his eyes and slowly shook his head.

With Paluntov nodding sympathetically, Andrei had forced himself to go on, "And I was in Kosovo when the first refugees were filmed by western media streaming out of the border. They were called Kosovars – even though they were Serbs fleeing Albanian looters and terrorists – because it did not fit the western story line. I fought against the white-robed jihadists, whom the western media called tragic fathers and sons from local towns, even though they had been recruited from around the world as a mercenary army. I saw political lies and horrible tragedies on all sides. This goes on without end. With all that, I cannot say that this has prepared me for these philosophical discussions. What good can come of polite philosophies when one experiences such horrors?

"If I do not have your academic training and experience of life, how can I make decisions that are the right ones? You will not be surprised that in my life decisions have been based on emotions and instant reactions. There was no time for sober thought. Is this not the normal state of affairs for most, if not all of us? How can I take time to have a philosophical thought about helping a friend who has been shot in the gut!" He shivered at the memory.

While Paluntov digested his earnest question, Andrei turned sharply to focus on the idyllic country scene spread out below him. Leaning next to Paluntov on the concrete balustrade, Andrei carried on, "Sir, it seems that you offer a circular argument. It appears that I cannot be trusted to make the right decisions until I have a full life's experience behind me; but, without that experience, I cannot make the right choices by which to attain the right experiences."

Paluntov had beamed. "Experience modified by academic understanding. Excellent! The inhumane actions you have witnessed are... too much like those I, too, have seen. Indeed, like so many of us have witnessed since time began. You must know that such are the actions of humans in extraordinary circumstances. This is a good start. By recognizing that those events are tragic and wrong you have made a strong beginning, my young friend!"

A waiter entered the patio with a tray of drinks. Paluntov stepped to the table to take a glass of orange juice. Andrei picked up a vodka and brought his glass back to his concrete perch.

Paluntov politely thanked the waiter. Keeping Andrei in his gaze, the waiter whispered something to Paluntov, then left as Paluntov quietly dismissed him with a nod. Settling back onto the balustrade with his glass, half turned toward Andrei, Paluntov explained, "The waiter says that the terrorists – I presume he means your army buddies – have been escorted off the premises. If you wish to follow them to get a ride back…"

Andrei contritely shakes his head, "Thank you, no. They will go to the nearest bar and convince themselves that they have successfully disrupted a bunch of crazy western sympathizers."

Paluntov grinned and continued, "You are making one wise choice after another tonight… What was your name, again?"

"Andrei Mikojevich Orlov, sir."

"Thank you, Andrei Mikojevich. So, you see, there are at least two missing factors. The context and the vector. The context of an event is critical, and different every time. Then, without knowing the direction of the path and an appropriate pace for you to take down that path, how can you know which of the many possible paths to take? Too many people end up looking like the butterflies out there fluttering by from one flower to another. You may not believe me at this time, but I will now tell you the simple answer. Your path will be the one that is lit, though not always as brightly as one might wish, by the knowledge of our fathers, as has been absorbed into your soul through your parents and teachers. A large part of this knowledge has been written by the prophets into our Holy Bible, and it has also been added to by philosophers like Aristotle, Dante, Lenin and Tolstoy. The writings of these philosophers will tell you the form of the long path."

With bowed head, Andrei wanted to believe. "Sir, if I have not really read Tolstoy, how can my soul be informed by his writings. And, besides, what did Moses or Abraham know of atomic power? How can their teachings be relevant?" He knew he shouldn't say this, but he couldn't help himself, "These terrible things I have seen makes me wonder if there really is a God."

Jumping right on the last consonant, Paluntov spoke harshly and clearly. "Dostoyevsky said this: If God does not exist, everything is permitted."

Paluntov paused to let it sink in.

"As to what the prophets may have seen, that is not the question. What they learned and tried to teach was not how to milk camels, but the value of a certain number of camels and to what ends they may be used. When an important decision must be made, you must first assess the reasons for making that decision. Ask *why*, then ask again, to dig deeper. If I were to say that we must take the car to go to Moscow, you should first ask for what purpose. It may be that a phone call will suffice."

Paluntov looked Andrei up and down. "Of course, you need to have been schooled in these matters, and I must admit that our modern schooling has strayed far from the considered, intelligent writings of our fathers. Their written words do not give *answers*, and, may I boldly say, nor were they intended to. It is the greater concepts that must be divined from the stories. Knowing how to understand what has been learned is the first stage of a proper education. At least, it should be." He paused again, as an academic would, to let his students catch up.

"History, philosophy and literature are now taught in an offhanded way as *subjects*, where one is expected to memorize facts, by which one obtains marks. This is not how these complex topics should be taught. What must be explained is the exposition, the diorama, the beautiful progression of the human mind over the ages, with one difficult lesson learned on top of the previous lessons. But that is another topic." He shook his head sadly.

"For those who have had the pleasure to study this, what our religious writings and great thinkers have given us must *not* be considered an absolute and prescriptive set of rules by which we are intended to slog through life, step after step. That was the blind, robot-like doctrine of Stalin. And that, too, is the substance of the childish religions of so much of Africa and the robber barons of the United States. They say, 'Have sex with a young girl to cure AIDS', or 'Accumulate more wealth and possessions to prove you are a worthy man before some god and your neighbours'. In well-considered philosophical arguments, young man, it is important that you have been shown how to develop a soul that sees the beauty of the long path, based on the experience of the souls of virtuous men before you."

Paluntov paused to look into the now darkening horizon. "We have so haltingly progressed from the tyranny of any one leader's megalomania, to an understanding that many individuals can, and wish to, and do, make decisions that contribute to the general welfare of all men. This progression is only possible when each generation passes on the better ideas they have learned, carefully considered, to the next generation." He glanced at Andrei's military-casual attire and added, "To a generation that has been properly schooled and prepared to understand these ideas."

Andrei noticed his prominent eyebrows knitting as Paluntov had turned to strain at movement in the line of trees that extended away from the rear of the old dacha. He felt a very strong desire to call him grandfather, wanting to protect him.

Seeing nothing in the trees, Andrei returned like a parched island castaway to drink of this philosophy. He asked, "How? Sir, how can my generation learn these things if are we so busy dodging bullets, crass advertising by gangsters, or scratching a living out of the meager dirt left us by those who have accumulated everything else. Even if I had time or the opportunity, how can I know *which* of so many thinkers are to be respected more than the others? And," before Paluntov could reply, "may I be so bold as to say, our generation has had some successes in changing our perspectives. You say 'men'…"

Paluntov sighed. "True, you have me with my older generation's pants down. '*People*', not just men." He smiles contritely. "And that advancement of knowledge is the very thing that I want to see!" Then, quietly, "And was hoping to see in some like you.

"Now, you ask more difficult questions, Andrei Mikojevich. Allow me to place before you your first lesson. I will tell you a secret about wine." He smiled at Andrei's quizzical take.

Pointing to the lush landscape, "If we were to plant grapes in this meadow, do you think the vines should flourish and produce luscious grapes?"

Andrei couldn't see any obvious traps. "Of course, sir. Though I'm not sure…"

"Ahah! You may ask any vintner the truth of this – if vines were planted here they would grow magnificently, with huge green leaves to catch the bright sun. But the grapes would be meager little after-thoughts. The reason is, there would be no incentive for the vines to send nourishment to their grape bunches, their seeds for future vines. The growth of their own vine trunks and leaves would receive all the attention. Now, if we plant vines on the poor soil up the side of a volcano, they would say to themselves, My God! We're in trouble here! Better make as many good grapes as we can, because we may not survive till next year! Those fruits, young man, are the ones we prize."

Letting that sink in, Paluntov continued, "And so it is with humanity. Harsh environments can produce the best fruit."

Andrei couldn't help adding, "Unless they're dead."

Paluntov gives a wry nod of agreement. "I must give you that. Now, back to the little question of, as the Englishman says, life, the universe and everything.

"I reluctantly admit to, ah, a way of cheating, shall I say. Philosophical cheating, if I may. I have asked myself these very types of questions and found my intelligence to be wanting." He held up a hand, adding quickly, "Yes, me. And, I say in my defence, there are precious few, ah, people alive now or in our past, who could do any better. This is hard. And you must accept that it is hard." He smiled. "It has taken me a long time to even approach an understanding. But, the closer I get, the greater I believe the reward will be." He looked down sheepishly. "I have this immodest feeling that there is something – something very important that is just beyond my reach. And it stays frustratingly just out there!" He pounded the concrete rail solidly once with his right hand, taking Andrei by surprise, causing him to jerk reflexively.

Stretching away from the concrete balustrade, Paluntov pulled out a pillowed chair from under an ornate, marble-topped, round table. "Let us sit down. My old bones can take only so much cold stone. Now – my method of cheating, which you may or may not find useful, is to look to the writings of thinkers like our own Tolstoy. I reasoned that if I found him in general to be likeable and virtuous, then perhaps his thinking corresponded to mine. This is one of my shortcuts and I make no apologies for it. For Tolstoy, religion had to do with our individual relationship with the world that we occupy... Do you understand? He and others have defined their view of religion. It is not fully the same as mine, and that does not matter, as I will explain. Yes, Tolstoy's was an anti-authoritarian view. Tolstoy made this further, and very difficult, addition to his philosophy:

what he thought may be irrelevant to you. He hoped that you would *not* follow what he said as some kind of gospel. He wanted you to search and extend the breadth your own conscience, so that you would develop your own way of defining your philosophy, reaching for a truly virtuous soul. He said this because he reasoned that if he didn't care for authoritarian strictures, how could he expect you to blindly follow *his* writings?"

Andrei slowly shook his head. "Sir, you have used virtue to describe what a good philosopher has. What is that? And, you have taken me around the same circle again and my head is spinning. This time the circle's name is conscience. The previous circle was called soul. And now you say it doesn't matter because I should make it up myself... "

They both sighed. Paluntov took Andrei's hand, holding it in both of his. A quiet bond was made as they saw deeper than the other's face.

Paluntov waved slowly toward the meadows they could see through the ornate concrete balustrade guarding the high patio. "Andrei, as I said, this is hard and I have not explained it well. That is why it should take so long, with competent professors in classrooms devoted to the subject. This late in the day, I admit that my powers of explanation are close to an ebb. And yet…" He finished his glass of juice, placing the glass on the table into a precise geometric location among the marble striations.

"Let me give you the short version. Your conscience does the active commenting on events as you see them. It helps you survive the daily flings at your attention and your mind. What you see every minute of every day does not usually need much thought. A car approaches, you avoid it. No moral decision needed. Then, you may see on the road an old woman who cannot avoid the car so easily. A decision is called for. Do you help this women cross the road? For many of us, we determine in a split second: is there danger; can I be effective in avoiding the danger; how would that affect me? should I do an altruistic act? Then, you make your decision." He smiled, "We will leave for later the much more difficult question of the 'runaway trolley problem'."

Andrei looked quizzical, but Paluntov carried on.

"Your *soul* is deeper, guiding the form and substance of your conscience. With a knowledge of what that form ought to look like, your conscience can be trained like a muscle to react automatically. For some, that training may be a long and difficult task. Indeed, if distracted by the compulsive accumulation of wealth, it may be stillborn."

Andrei had let out a short, "Hah!"

"Exactly. So now, with a virtuous soul having trained your conscience you can observe an event and know with minimal rational analysis that it may make you indignant, or appreciative, as the case may be."

Pleased with himself, Paluntov had leaned toward Andrei. "Let me give you a current example of how my conscience made such a choice based on my soul." Glancing back at the door to make sure they were alone, the Director explained, "My conscience has been troubled by a favourite new term from President Putin – 'Novorossiya'".

Andrei remembered thinking it was an extraordinary act of courage by the Director to say that.

Paluntov was reawaken by the topic. "Does your conscience feel the same about that charged word, when you allow your conscience to speak? Myself, I take with a bitter grain of salt what our present leader is saying. He is throwing away all pretense of any relaxation of the yolk of power held by the Kremlin over the proletariat. His actions crush the principles of our great philosophers, of individual thought, and of rational action in favour of accumulation of power and wealth. Rather than considering the concept that a people free to live without corruption and despotic bureaucrats, is a people free to invent and progress; no, he uses *Novorossiya* to crassly return to totalitarianism and the pogroms of Stalin. Beware of that fake jingoism, my young friend. We must have a more constant faith to guide our decision-making. The teachings of our long-established philosophies provides nourishment and sustenance for my soul, and, growing out of that understanding, my own conscience is my guide past the daily fads of politically self-serving ideologues."

He peered closely at Andrei. "If you did allow your conscience to have a say, what would you think?" He paused while Andrei collected himself. "You do not have to answer me, Andrei Mikojevich. I insist, however, that you must answer yourself."

This respected old fellow had made a profound impression on Andrei. Up to that day, he had been caught up in the simple story lines of *Mother Russia against the world*. During the rest of that evening's discussions downstairs, Andrei hardly listened. He was reassessing in his mind what he really did think. Andrei realized that in the several careers that he had gone

through, he was always trying to create a new "Andrei".
He had felt his flexibility was a positive characteristic.
Now...

So, years later, Director Paluntov was to bring Andrei
his official papers allowing him to perform good deeds in
the Arctic. Paluntov arrived at his apartment with a
bureaucrat called Juri Gherov. Andrei was nervously
vacillating between wanting to welcome an admired
father-figure and worrying that the authorities would jail
him for something.

They had met in the dingy, poorly-lit lobby of
Andrei's low-class standard grey concrete block of an
apartment building. Andrei had been prepared to visit
the Institute's office but Director Paluntov clearly did not
want others from his facility present at this meeting.
Unknown to Andrei, until later, the bureaucrat who
came with Paluntov had forced himself into the meeting.

Befitting an important and respected senior official,
Paluntov was dressed in an expensive dark suit. His
white hair overflowed at the side, giving him an
academic look.

Gherov's polyester suit would, no doubt, be wrinkle-resistant. His gaunt face, thin black hair and small frame made the grey suit look slapped on.

Gherov's compulsion of playing with his cellphone was quite distracting. He was a nervous man who constantly sniffed. He could be heard coming before he was seen.

Nevertheless, Andrei refocused, and addressed Paluntov, as the obviously senior representative. "I am deeply honoured, Director, that you should come to speak with me." He was about to perform a respectful embrace.

Before he could, Gherov jumped in the away, taking over. With hands clasped firmly around his phone, as if it was an official talisman, he went into a canned speech that sounded like it came directly from the bowels of the Kremlin. He seemed to wield some political power that was not apparent from his title of Operations Advisor.

After several minutes of boring politbureau-speak, Gherov paused to catch his breath. Paluntov grasped the opportunity to step forward to shake Andrei's hand warmly, trying to impress on Gherov that the two had a valued friendship. "Your service in the Army was with distinction, Andrei Mikojevich, and we have noted that you are a strong supporter of our Holy Orthodox Church." He winked at Andrei with that statement. Andrei picked up immediately that Gherov was not "one of them". Andrei could see a tension between them. Andrei didn't trust the slyness that exuded from the younger official.

With the mention of the church, Paluntov and Andrei had blessed themselves in unison.

The two deliberately waited until Gherov slipped his omnipresent phone into a pocket and fumbled through the four-point blessing.

Paluntov carried on, "We encourage your enthusiasm in this project, Andrei Mikojevich. Young people must have a variety of experiences so they can mature into wise leaders." He winked again, making Andrei uncomfortable. Without Gherov there, he knew they would have had a long and interesting talk.

Juri Gherov showed clear impatience with pleasantries. Junior though he was, Gherov insisted on carrying the conversation. After a few more tries at speaking, with Gherov talking over him, Paluntov politely sat back.

Gherov informed Andrei, "Right. Now, allow me to tell you a little-noted fact in this time of critical change.

The lands of far Siberia are becoming of very great significance, geopolitically. Mother Russia and our Church are under great pressure from foreign enemies. The Church from the 'Stans of the south, and the integrity of our homeland from terrorists, western capitalists and gangsters from our past." In saying the mantra, he glanced at Paluntov, sniffed, then carried on. "The eternal ice of the Arctic is melting. You may know that recently it has become apparent that our Arctic coast is open for more tanker routes."

Paluntov jumped in to add, "This may be good news for selling our oil and other resources to Europe, but our great back door is getting drafty. The Canadian and American coasts are not yet so drafty."

Hesitating, Gherov found his place again. "Quite so, Director. We must know what the Canadian infrastructure really looks like now, and whether there are threats from the loud barking toy poodles in that direction. When their ice melts permanently, they will have a competing route to Europe for Chinese and Indian trade. It will cost us control and money." He gave a short significant nod and a sniff to Andrei.

Despite what Andrei had first presumed to be a simple handover of papers, Andrei quickly saw why at least Gherov was here. There was business to be done. "You already have satellite pictures and probably a lot more, sir. What do you need from me, sitting in a backwater Arctic village?"

Pawn to Rook two. Gherov sighed. "Good question, my friend. It is good to see that you can think clearly." He smiled slyly and sniffed, stretching out his words for emphasis. "You are right, Andrei Mikojevich. We probably do not need you in that place. So, in that case, you do not qualify for the government subsidy for foreign work." He saw Andrei's raised eyebrows and the wry smile from Paluntov, and, "I will have to check on this visa. It may not be correct, now…" He ended with an expectant cock of the head.

Seeing where those moves led, Andrei bowed in defeat. "So what do you want me to do?"

Gherov paused to study Andrei. "Well… You may be of some small assistance after all. I have to return to Moscow for a meeting tomorrow, but I will, ah, ask Director Paluntov to bring you a device. He can take it through his diplomatic bag to Canada. It looks like a rock…"

CORPORATE **M & A**

Farmer's back forty

Amongst the routine garbage dump that the farm had been using for years as a midden, there is the car-sized cylinder of a large propane-powered burner being fired up by a confident young man. Sandy is dressed in a mixture of expensive runners and dark brown leather jacket with top-of-the-line distressed jeans and a muscle-shirt.

He looks at his phone for the time. Shakes his head.

"Curly and Mo bloody-well better get here soon or I'll charge them for the extra propane."

In a few minutes an older SUV bumps along the farm lane, swerving to avoid potholes. The vehicle pulls up near Sandy and the burner, then backs toward it with Sandy giving perfunctory hand signals.

Sandy yells out, "Fine! Close enough."

Curly opens the driver's door to slowly drop out his large legs. He labours to extract his corpulent body from the seat. Mo is already out and opening the rear hatch. He waits impatiently for Curly to waddle back to help.

"Come on, Curly, for fucksake. It's gonna rain by the time you get here!" Mo looks up at the dark clouds.

Sandy smiles at the scene. Still grinning, he opens the burner's large door as Mo and Curly shuffle up to the burner. Mo is carrying the light end of a body wrapped tightly in large garbage bags. He pushes as Curly stuffs the head and shoulders into the fire. Curly jumps away from the blast of heat then helps Mo maneuver the rest of the body into the fire.

Finished with their task, Curly and Mo wipe their hands symbolically on their pants as they turn to their SUV. Mo pulls the hatch closed. Sandy adjusts the heat up in the burner. He peeks in through a glass hole to check on the flame.

Satisfied, Sandy steps down to Mo, who already has his hand out.

Without a word, Sandy pulls an envelope from his back pocket and hands it to Mo.

Curly smiles at the envelope. "Glad to do business with you, Bro."

Sandy nods then dismissively turns to tend to the burner.

Mo plops into his seat to wait for Curly to insert himself behind the steering wheel. They drive off.

Spying sideways at the departing vehicle, Sandy starts to say, "Goo... Shit," as the SUV stops suddenly then comes bouncing backwards recklessly through the potholes. First out is a fuming Curly. He stomps ominously toward Sandy.

"What the fuck you trying to pull here?"

Mo catches up to him waving a handful of twenty dollar bills and the ripped-open envelope. "We're short five bills, man! What's going on?"

Sandy pretends to adjust the burner then turns to face them. "Huh? What do you mean short?"

He takes the reluctantly proffered bills to count them.

"Oh fuck. You're right guys. Hey! I'm really sorry. Must have mixed up the envelopes. Here. Let me give you the hundred." He hands back the bills and reaches, plainly, for his wallet. Sandy counts out five twenties and gives them to Mo. "Really sorry, Mo. I would've made it up next time. That envelope was supposed to go to the farmer. Honest. No bad feelings?"

Curly is still glaring but Mo nods. "All good. You ought to mark the envelopes or something."

Sandy nods, "Yeah. Probably should. Can't use Mo and Curly. How about I use, like, the Brothers Grim?"

Mo smiles. "The Brothers Grim. I like it!" He gives Sandy the secret handshake, as does a confused Curly.

Seated again in the SUV, Curly looks at Mo. "What's with the Grim shit?"

"Oh shut up Curly. What would you know about high-brow literature?"

They drive away, leaving a disappointed Sandy.

Later, Sandy is satisfied with the state of the remains in his cooled burner. He carefully scrapes and brushes the ashes into a biodegradable bag. Rain starts splattering on the metal awning overhead. Using an umbrella to protect the bag of ashes, he carries it to his sporty sedan. The trunk lid lifts to his command and he places the bag into a plastic crate. The lid shuts itself as he backs away. With rain becoming heavier, Sandy closes up the burner's box and controls with separate locks then hurries to his car.

Seated, contemplating the pouring rain, he goes over some options. "Already done the little bridges too much. Can't leave tracks by the canal in this rain. Have to go up 3, past Hope. There's that logging road by the river. Nice drive."

Having made his decision Sandy fires up the big engine. He guns it, making the tires skid, then crawls along the lane to avoid bottoming out.

On the highway he calls up his cousin. "Hey Deep! How's tricks?"

"She's fine, Sandy. What's up?"

"Hey Bro, chill out. Just driving the latest to his rest."

"Shut the fuck up, Sandy. What do you want?"

Pausing for a minute to calm his cousin down, "Listen Deep, I need some help."

"No money. Told you. You have to earn it."

"Of course, cous'. That's all I want. To earn it. But I need a bit more just now. Listen. Let me pick up the next one..."

"No fucken way! You know how this works! Each guy does his own shit and nobody can follow the trail. For fucksake! I knew you'd mess up... You using again?"

"No no. Honest. Deep. It's just a few stocks that I was, ah, trading, and I need to cover them by the day after tomorrow. Morning."

"Stocks. You?"

"Well, yeah. Like, why not me?"

"What stocks?"

"Well, like, ok. It makes no difference if you invest, too. I got a special tip. There's this gold mining operation that's going to start in, well near, Kamloops. The property owner..."

"Sandy, I don't want to hear this. Gold mine, eh? Kamloops. When you're done with that I can sell you a few shares in a bridge I've got in Manhattan. No money. You earn your way to bankruptcy like the rest of us."

"Deep. Let me speak, please. All I want is to make the next pickup myself. Don't call Mo, call me. Just this once. You said you had a special tomorrow night?"

Pause.

"Ah fuck, Sandy. Not this one."

"You know my lips are sealed..."

"Not this one. Sorry, no."

Tomorrow night, Sandy is helping his cousin with a bag.

"Do not. I repeat. DO NOT take the bag off his head!"

Of course, Sandy pulls too hard and the bag slips down to the body's shoulders.

"Oh my god, Deep! Not him. He, he's the guy that pays us!"

"Shut up, Sandy. Just help me with his gold fillings."

Sandy hands Deep a pair of pliers and blue gloves from a box.

"Corporate merger, Sandy. He was in the way. What can I say? I just shut up and take orders like you're supposed to. Right?... RIGHT?"

LIVING IN A PINGO

The two make a fashion statement walking on the crumbling runway, with their tanned leather fur-lined hoods, bright oversized coveralls and bulky government-approved thermal construction boots. Simion walks awkwardly on the gravel of the neglected Arctic airport. His boot heels seem to hit too soon, throwing off his normal gait. On the walk along the perimeter of the runway, he takes every opportunity to stop to investigate something, thereby giving his calves a rest.

Andrei waits for a minute at one point to mention something he thought about. "Sun stay high for long time. Will be hours before it rest."

Simion is grateful for the conversation, "Oh yeah! Forgot about the extra daylight. We'll have lots of time to settle in."

Wandering around in the orange coveralls, getting the lay of the land, Andrei feels uncomfortable in the open. He decides to follow a trail that was tramped through the gravelly muskeg and the amazingly persistent grasses. The path could have been made either last week or a thousand years ago. Andrei stops in surprise as he sees the path going from the airport site down to a beautiful, regular dome of muskeg that is located in a large protected shelf, just below the level of the upper plain. He stands admiring the dome.

Meanwhile on the upper level, Simion stops to pick at the dry lichen that clings to one side of a rock, feigning interest in the stubborn growth.

A glint of sun reflects off something behind a distant mound, behind Simion.

A young man from town, Mikey, has his new binoculars trained on Simion. He can't see Andrei any more. As he cautiously follows Simion disappearing lower down the slope, Mikey steps slowly out into the open.

Curiosity has the better of Andrei as he proceeds down the steep slope of mixed muskeg and worn gravel. Near the bottom he takes in the symmetry of the dome. He thinks that it must be man-made.

At the bottom, Andrei calls out, "Simion! Here is round building! Or cave…"

Nearby now, Simion decides to bound down the steep path to join him. He playfully jumps higher than he normally would, and with the wind pushing his back strongly, Simion feels like he is jumping on the moon. Andrei stands patiently pointing at an oval hole in the base of the muskeg dome. The opening is partially covered by a torn door. Smiling at Simion's attempt to get airborne, he yells, "Is maybe home to bear, no? Where is gun?"

Simion slides awkwardly to an emergency stop on the loose gravel of the path. "Shit! You're right! Back out of here, Andrei. The rifle's in the tent."

Heads down into their furry parkas, they jog with determination into the gale that is now in their face as they make their way back to their bright yellow tent. They don't see Mikey madly scrambling back to the cover of a tall mound.

Heavy plodding in the awkward boots are causing Simion's calves to cramp up. Near their tent, he stops, leaning down to rub his sore legs.

He barely notices that the tent is being tossed about and that its sides are flapping noisily. He does notice a distant engine sound, lifting his head for an instant to check it out. But Andrei grabs his attention with one of his new words, "Shit", pointing at the wallowing tent. A stake has pulled out, allowing the whole tent to do its crazy dance.

Simion raises his eyebrows at their almost airborne sleeping quarters. Without the boxes inside, it would have been gone. It dawns on them both that they will have to live in this thing.

Speaking loudly over the flapping racket, "Andrei, I don't know if I'm more worried about this tent becoming a kite while we sleep, or being visited by a bear down in that cave." He nods at the nearby wall remnants of the old airport buildings. "Those things are just as likely to fall on us at any time... And we could be safer in the cave."

Andrei undoes the tent door straps, puts a foot inside to steady it while Simion retrieves their rifle. "Is maybe better to fix door for cave before we sleep."

"You know, Andrei, let's do that. Have to see if we can get our stuff inside the place. I have a feeling that's where the previous crew must have been sleeping anyway. Why don't we take our tool box down there and see what's needed?"

He looks toward the village. "Did you hear something from out there?"

"Too busy. What hear?"

"Thought it was a snowmobile..."

Andrei stands up to stare along the intervening muskeg. Nothing but tundra. He shrugs. "Use sled to take boxes to cave."

Through the rising gale, the cave door gets repaired. They work with resolve to haul all of their boxes and equipment down to the lower level with their sled, then they settle into the domed cave. A catalytic stove starts to shed some heat and tiny rays of light on the interior. They keep their coats on.

Sitting on two old aluminum folding chairs that had been tied to one of the walls up on the airfield, the two adventurers catch their breath, trying to feel comfortable in their new abode.

An LED light reflects off the crystal-frozen wall. Its unnatural bluish light distorts distances in the cave. Simion grumbles, "I can't read by this stupid light."

He gets up to drag one of the heavy boxes to the door, which opens inward. Cracking the door open a bit, Simion props the box against it to hold it slightly in the gale. The box isn't up to the task, getting steadily pushed in over the frozen sand floor by the swirling gusts. Andrei pointedly puts his hood on, to protect against the cold.

Standing over the box like a stern father, Simion encourages it to cooperate. "Stay, damnit!" It doesn't. "Ah to hell with it!" Simion pushes the door shut, kicks the box out of the way, and stomps over to his chair.

Flipping back his hood, Andrei mumbles, "Box need training, or shooting."

Without really hearing that, Simion picks up the rifle leaning against his chair.

"Andrei, why don't you take the rifle. I want to get close to that damn light so I can read something."

Hefting the rifle then checking the magazine and safety, "Ok, my friend. You read love story? Already lonely for Vancouver girl?"

Simion drags his aluminum chair over to the box that now serves as their main table. Wriggling his coat-covered hips down between the wooden arms, he opens up the book.

He grins, "No, you horny Russian. This is the book they gave us about Arctic survival. Might come in handy."

"What means horny Russian?" He peers suspiciously at Simion.

"Horny means you'd rather have a lovely blond model in this cave, instead of me."

"Is true. Now. But after month…" He pretends to leer at Simion.

Simion flips pages. "Forget it, Rasputin. Try the bears… Oh!" He reads ahead from the book.

"Change your mind?"

"Huh? No, listen. We're in a pingo."

"Is word from Australia?"

"No, no. The book's talking about these things that are huge bubbles that push up the permafrost. Methane accumulation in the muskeg and perma-ice upthrust makes them. In this area, could be as much as thirty metres around, it says. A pingo. How do you like that? We're living in a pingo!"

"Feel like kangaroo pouch, for sure... Bloody cold pouch." Andrei fingers the cross that hangs inside his sweater, mumbles something with eyes raised, then blesses himself.

After a while, Andrei lays out his sleeping bag on one of the pieces of ragged plywood they scavenged from the buildings. "Wood is more better than plastic on ground. Not so cold." They both nod at that.

Simion puts his book away. Unfurling their sleeping bags, Simion takes time to add in another loose blanket that extends the end of the bag to make up for his height.

After learning how to warm up food and tea with a ceramic stove, they settle down for their first night on the tundra, each on their piece of plywood, bundled tightly against the cold.

Outside, the gale gets colder and more turbulent. While the door is in the lee, heavy air buffets and swirls back against the door, shaking it like a giant wanting in. The two environmentalists stare at the door between fitful bouts of snoring. A party of giants wanting into the cave wakes Andrei during some particularly loud snores from Simion. His eyes wide, he wraps a hand reassuringly around the stock of the rifle. "Bozhe moi." He reaches awkwardly through the sleeping bag to bless himself.

Getting back to sleep is helped by calm thoughts of the dacha where he first met Paluntov. Andrei thinks, *"This can be defined as a special experience, for sure. Is it going to help me make better decisions? I ask God,"* he blesses himself, *"for guidance."*

SKYTRAIN DESULTORY

A dark brown leather computer case sits strapped to the back of a quickly-striding older man. Under the wide strap, his beige golf-shirt is unbuttoned at the top. A moist umbrella is folded in his hand. He takes the Skytrain steps two at a time, his younger-looking wife easily keeping up with him.

She has on a bright yellow raincoat and her flat white loafers have rain stains. They help each other with clasped hands. They exchange a few whispers, taking in the human scenery on the approach to the station.

A silver cellphone clipped to his side rings. He puts it to his ear with a practiced move.

"Hello? … Peter! How are you? … Just bussing back from a client in Burnaby… Yes, the new graphic arts startup… They're looking for sixty-five million… Sure, the Taverna on Denman would be fine… See you tonight, then."

Each pull out their transit passes with a free hand; they swipe side-by-side and walk past a Skytrain guard who ignores them. He is looking for miscreants. They quickly head for opening car doors. Squeezing by two teenage boys who occupy the doorway, the older man confirms with a pat that his cellphone is clipped safely to his belt.

There are only a few other passengers in the car.

He nods slightly for his wife to look at the seats next to them, where a homeless man is slumped with his head fully down between his knees, in "crash position". A rough-cut middle-aged woman next to him is sitting by the window. They are dressed in a clean but odd assortment of clothes.

Using an economical shrug of his shoulder, the older man swings the heavy computer bag to his front and sits down in one of the bright orange seats that face forward, bag on his lap. His wife takes the aisle seat, placing her white, multi-zippered purse securely in her lap.

A young musician, dressed in black, boards the car just as the doors close. He carries a fine-tooled leather black box that holds bongo drums. The musician takes the seat across the aisle from the businessman and his wife, facing them. Noticing the slumped homeless man behind him, he puts both arms over his black box.

The rough-cut woman speaks to her companion in a quiet, raspy, tense voice that is ready for an explosion, "There's someone sitting in front of you sweety... *Cough cough.*"

The homeless man's answer emanates from the floor, "Uhm."

She continues. "*Cough*. Sweety, don't forget to ask him for a carton of cigarettes, ok?"

A rough, muffled answer comes from his sleeve. "Why are you bothering me every five minutes with that?"

"I'm sorry sweety. *Cough*. Are you going to remember to ask him?"

"Um?"

"Are you?"

"You're getting me mad!"

"I'm sorry, honeykins… Are you going to remember? *Cough cough*."

"Yeah."

The Skytrain car speaks, "Next stop is 29th Street."

"Sweety, the next stop is 29th Street."

"Uhm."

"Sweety, did he say he was going to meet you there? *Cough*"

"Uhm."

The train stops smoothly. The two young people who were standing in the doorway finally decide to sit down. A young man in red sneakers gets on. He sees the musician, recognizing him.

"Hey, Mickey!"

The musician looks up.

"Hi, Benny! How are you?"

Red sneakers-Benny sits across from the musician, facing the still slouched-over homeless man across the aisle.

The woman continues her interrogation, "Where?"

The homeless man mumbles dully, "Granville."

"Granville?"

"Burrard."

"Are you sure?

"Patterson."

"Do you remember, Sweety?"

"Waterfront."

"Honeykins, do you remember where he said he'd meet you?"

"Broadway."

The Skytrain announces, "Next stop, Stadium."

She persists, "*Cough.* Another stop. Sweety, don't forget to ask him to buy the cigarettes, ok?"

He doesn't move, "Will you stop bothering me?"

"Will you remember?"

A shoulder twitches, "Yes!"

Red sneakers-Benny shifts in his seat, "Got a gig, Mickey?"

Mickey looks up at one of the ads above the windows, "Just jammin'. Going to Vanney's. He has a great little studio." Mickey lifts up his black box to show it. He fondles it absently, listening to his mind's ear.

"You don't have to have a big place or anything, now. It's in his house – he has all the electronics you need. And what he calls it his *Padded Room*. Sound-proofed." Mickey grins.

Red sneakers nods, "You with a band?"

"Yeah. Well, we only did one session together, but it really clicked."

The Skytrain cuts in, "Next stop is Broadway."

Mickey gets up to leave. "I think this is really going to work out." An ad for Lotto 649 is behind his head.

Red sneakers nods at Mickey and the ad, "Yeah. Good luck. Really! See you around, Mickey!"

"See you, man."

The woman looks around to see where they are, "*Cough cough.*"

And the train rolls on.

DO THEY WALK AMONG US?

Aliens are already here. They have been here long before homo sapiens walked out of Africa (any of the times).

They look just like regular folks. Despite having been mostly killed off by now, the few secret survivors have remained quiet, peaceful and nice. That was their problem.

An analogy: chimpanzees have very close cousins called bonobos. Living peacefully in loose matriarchies, bonobos happily forage for their vegetarian meals, supplemented by a few tasty grubs; they use tools as needed; and they pass on cultural knowledge with a complex language. When occasional disputes arise in the extended family, they cuddle and make up.

Except for the regular cuddling, chimps are similar. However, in each chimp tribe, the prime male and his buddies can have an attitude. Every once in a while they get a red glare in their eyes. The boss and his pack start yelling and throwing branches around then go off on a testosterone-fueled hunting trip. They corral a hapless monkey, tear him limb from limb and gorge themselves with bloody meat.

Mother Nature's rule of survival of the most aggressive selects for those who eat the most bloody meat.

While neandertals were larger-brained than homo sapiens, my ancestors assure me they were more like bonobos. They did catch and eat large prey but where they could, they preferred their veggies.

The downfall of neandertals came about because, in addition to the new diseases brought by their cousins, they were nice. Like gorillas, the only time their eyes showed a red glare was when they were wronged by an outsider. This happened too often by those new groups of homo sapiens that marched into their area.

Over thousands of years of interaction and interbreeding, neandertal clans succumbed to the chimp-like trait exhibited by homo sapiens punk-packs, to get their testosterone-fueled rocks off.

Since neandertals lost the human race, the only thing left of them now is in the 1-4% of non-African genetic code.

However, every once in a while, across the gene pool, a neandertal pops up. Most are reflexively killed or ostracized by punk-packs of homo sapiens. Neither side knows why they do it. The response comes from deep genetic memory - like fear of wolves or snakes. Without knowledge of why he or she is bullied to death, the neandertal bows down to the punk-pack and either expires or retreats from the world in other ways. Some do music, drugs, or write.

As the winners in the human race, homo sapiens demonizes the losers. Neandertals are branded as knuckle-dragging cave-dwellers who could barely grunt enough words to alert another one about an approaching Mastodon.

The victors write the histories.
What were neandertals really like? May I suggest, from experience, that they preferred a peaceful family tribe whose eldest and wisest grandmother would be listened to with respect. And she, too, would listen to the young folks, respectfully. If a disagreement arose, it was talked out; at the end, the debaters hugged; and the family went on with battling the outside forces of the environment. Creativity was cherished. Myths and magic in the world were interwoven with the news brought by travelers, and all was retold at the fireside so everyone could enjoy the music and stories and learn from them.

There was very little room for error, with every other creature battling for life and the environment throwing up extreme weather changes and random eruptions of volcanoes messing up the scenery. When someone suggested to the matriarch a way to move forward, all the wise folk added their thoughts. The resulting decision was communally considered, but all agreed that it was the matriarch who would finally state the direction of the thing to be done.

And so it was for over 500,000 years. Neandertals lived on by following the principles of respect, creativity and wise decision-making.

Then along came the homo sapiens. It took a quick 50,000 years for the testosterone-fueled punk-packs to eliminate their rivals in the human race. They not only eliminated the families, they soiled the memory of the "nice humans". Eradicated to such an extent that even the rare neandertal who pops up through the gene pool is made to feel ashamed of being somehow "different" and inferior.

What is happening now? The elite homo sapiens punk-packs are spinning ever tighter into their gated communities of one-percenters – leaving the rest of their own kind on the outside – perhaps those few of us neandertals who have survived by pretending to be human can join with the 99-percenters barred outside the gates.

Perhaps we can teach the value of *respect, creativity and wise decision-making.* Perhaps we should all just leave the one-percenters alone within their glittering little gated worlds. If we all walk away from them, they can rattle their self-imposed bars as much as they want.

Just don't force us into a red-eyed glare.

-a neoandertal

VISITOR

Over the days, Simion and Andrei spend most of their time chased into their pingo by the ever-present freezing gale.

The next morning brings a better day. While on reconnaissance to map out the locations of toxic dump sites, Simion sees young Mikey sitting on his snowmobile. Unnoticed in the gale, Simion walks up behind him. He sees that Mikey is using a sharp knife to slice off a chunk of meat from a fresh-killed and skinned seal's hind quarter.

At a scraping sound from Simion, Mikey startles and cuts himself. He throws a dirty cloth over the seal parts, then sticks his bleeding thumb in his mouth. Spinning around, he holds the knife in his right hand, looking like he is ready to use it on Simion.

Simion takes a step back, raising his arms. "Hey Mikey, I'm really sorry! I didn't mean to surprise you like that! Can I help? Let me help you bandage…"

Mikey pulls his thumb out of his mouth to say, "Bugger off! What the hell you doing sneaking around here like that? Owww!"

"I can…"

"NO! Bugger off!" He puts his thumb back in his bloody mouth and waves the knife with his free hand.

With a shrug, Simion backsteps and heads off toward his next possible dump inspection site. Looking back occasionally, he sees Mikey awkwardly wrap things up then get his snowmobile going. Simion hears it for a minute, then it stops. With another shrug, "Well, I offered. What the hell's he doing there, anyway?"

After finishing, Simion tromps back to the cave and quickly slams the newly reinforced rough-hewn door behind him into total darkness. The inside of the door is cold and slimy. He wipes his hand on the leg of his coveralls. As his eyes adjust, faded green symbols come into view on a small electronic device beyond his reach. Shining sharply from the door, two thin lines of light mark the floor in front of him with a distorted right-angle. He steps forward, blocking off most of the horizontal line with his shoulders.

Something stirs nearby.

Simion stops. "That you Andrei?"

The Russian accent answers, "Yes, of course, my friend. Think maybe I am bear?"

Simion snorts as he shuffles ahead toward the shadow of a chair. "Ha! You? You're a pussycat, Andrei.

Not anything like a friggen bear." His eyes adjusting, he catches a glimpse of gleaming teeth near the green light.

Simion steps carefully in the dark. Speaking as much to keep Andrei located, he says, "This is going to be one hell of a vacation, old man. That weird kid was out on his snowmobile, over by sector 2D. He cut his finger when I came up behind him."

"Hunting?"

"Not around here, unless he can do something with a lemming. No, he had a seal carcass he must've caught from the shore. "

"Hunting for lemming soup?"

Simion laughs, "You'd need ten for one bowl!" He tries to coax some heat out of the little ceramic stove into his hands. "He was cutting the seal up. Maybe trying to trap foxes. No idea what he was doing."

He sees Andrei is sorting markers by colour, holding each one into a ray of light to confirm what it says is its colour.

"Do you think those special markers are going to do the job on the barrels? Even frozen?"

"Should. Tested by expert. Graffiti artist friend say they mark all thing."

"So why didn't our government guy, Mike-the-other, provide us with something? And maybe a real house, too."

Simion plops down awkwardly into the aluminum tube chair. His bulky clothing catches on the wooden arms, clamping his body into the chair.

He wiggles his bum for some room then heaves a sigh. "Did you get through to the Institute?" Simion's frigid breath hangs in front of him in a dark shadowy cloud. Unseen, Andrei rolls his eyes at the question.

The howling wind outside continues its battering at the door. As Simion's eyes adjust better he sees that he did not latch the door well enough. Mini whirlwinds whip up the frigid snowdust, framed by light from a weak and lowering sun, coming in around the door. Puffs of steam from his mouth hang for a brief instant in front of his face. Simion gets up, again catching the armrest with his coat, which hauls the chair up like it was stuck to his bum. The aluminum chair rattles against the hard sand floor as he shakes it from his rear end, then he stomps to the door. Pushing hard against the door with a shoulder, Simion gets the latch all the way down. It's now darker and a bit quieter. He wipes the slime off both hands onto his legs.

The smell of cold musty dirt gets up Andrei's nose. He sneezes.

"Simion, did tent live? Could see through blizzard?"

Opening up the coat's zippers before sitting back down, Simion shakes his head. "Nope. Couldn't even see the tatters."

He looks around. "If this pingo bubble wasn't here we'd be polar popsicles for sure! So much for boss Mike's assurance that we'd be as comfortable as possible."

Andrei snorts. "What mean, possible?" He reaches for the electronic device. "Try Oceanographic Institute in Vladivostok, and try Mountain Police channel. Are different time zone, yes?"

An exasperated nod from Simion shakes the fur hood that is half off his head. "The RCMP detachment isn't staffed all the time but they should be there now."

"So some person should be awake now, yes?"

Simion nods. "Whoever was left in charge by Mike is not doing his job! He would go to a place like Africa and leave us in this deep freeze!" Rubbing his hands briskly, Simion reaches for a pot of tea to pour some into a metal cup.

Mumbling, "Ice tea," he sighs in exasperation at the low heat setting that Andrei insists they use, to conserve supplies.

Louder, "Need to warm this up again, eh?" He takes a long slurp. The lukewarm liquid is welcome, anyway. He settles back as comfortably as he can into the aluminum-frame chair. Its original wooden back-slats have long ago been replaced by rough-cut aluminum strips from the wings of a crashed airplane. But aluminum is colder than wood.

"This storm, I think, is being pushed by the jet-stream loop up through the Arctic. Could be disrupting reception."

"Sense makes." Andrei shrugs. "So what we do? Need more antenna? When come supply plane? Need heat! No tree outside mean we freeze when all fuel can go empty!" He tosses an arm toward a plastic-wrapped package of fuel cans.

Simion shifts under his layers of clothing. "Our time zone..." He wrinkles his brows. "Vladivostok is, what, plus 12 Zulu?" A nod from Andrei. "And we're at minus 8, no, minus 4 here. Vancouver is minus 8 Zulu, right?"

Andrei reaches for his non-existent cellphone. "Yebem..." he mutters. "Do not know. Sound good."

Something rolls down the ramp in front of their abode and slaps into the door and its dirt support. More snowdust gets kicked off the curved wall/ceiling, swirling slowly with the eddies, lighting up in the few rays of luminescence from the transmitter, along with the clouds of their breaths. Both their wide eyes shine, too, straining to see in the dark. Simion shakes head, refocusing on their predicament. Andrei sneezes loudly.

Simion says, "Bless you."

Andrei blesses himself. "Damn dirt! And mould! It stink! Is like, like baba's potato hole!"

Simion smiles. "Fruit cellar. You can always step outside, my friend. Our tent is well past the airport, by now, heading for Pelly Bay. Might have to go to their church after all, eh?"

"Not Mikey's church." Frustrated, Andrei wipes his nose broadly with the sleeve of his sweater that sticks out past the orange coveralls. He tries to read one of his cyrillic-printed books. An Orthodox cross on the cover is the only thing Simion recognizes.

Rousing himself to action, Simion raises his voice. "Andrei, we need to figure out when we can call at the right time. They probably think we're out tagging ptarmigans and friggen white foxes, playing in the sand!" He kicks at the mixture of frozen dirt and blond sand on the floor.

Opening up his zippers a bit more, Simion stares at the ceiling. "Ok. We've been in this dungeon for over 70 hours, so it's Thursday, ah… afternoon! Well into so-called May, up here. Andrei, have you tried all the channels on the phone?"

Nodding, Andrei gestures at the transmitter. "Do not hear from Elena for many week. Make me worry." He stretches toward Simion with the radio. "Elena will bring my money and I live in condo in Coal Harbour." His bright smile shows clearly.

"You mean the one in Nunavut?"

"NO not Coal Harbour in Nunavut…"

As Simion reaches for the transmitter the door bursts open blinding them both. He yells in fear. Bitterly cold air rushes at them.

With snowdust flying, a terrifyingly big polar bear settles down onto both front paws, grins at Simion, then moves quickly through the doorway, slashes at Simion's outstretched arm and is about to open her mouth over his neck when BANG!

Andrei shoots again BANG!

The bear roars and rises toward full height slamming her head against the ceiling BANG!

Reddened across her chest, she crumples onto the floor, snowdust and chunks of dirt rain down from the ceiling onto her white fur. Her splayed-out left paw pushes hard on Simion's left arm. He can't get it away. The bent chair still holds him awkwardly, along with the great paw. She drags her paw slowly, with Simion's arm, toward her head. Simion's glasses are clouded by the final breath escaping from the great bear, as he and his chair scrape in slow-motion closer to her huge teeth. Incongruously, he notices that the paw's skin is black under the white fur.

Snapping his body straight out of the chair and from under her paw, Simion frantically scrambles away, pressing well into the frozen dirt wall as far away as he can from the mother polar bear.

Staring through the smashed door, in the howling snow-gale, Simion's desperate eyes scan the ramp that leads up from the cave. A very young cub peeks around the top of the ramp, then gives a quiet yelp. It backs away out of sight into the gale.

Andrei is on his knees, pressed against the dark wall on the other side of the cave. His rifle is held chest-high, ready for another shot at the reddening white mass on their floor. "B-bozhe moi!" Feeling the heat of the bear on his face, Andrei brushes at his cheek with his right hand, then quickly pulls the rifle stock back up to position.

Simion starts to shake, sending a light halo of snowdust off the wall behind him. "Andrei! K-keep your gun on him!"

A widening pool of blood soaks into the floor around the bear.

Gruffly, "Think is dead, Simion. Move paw – see if he lives."

Pushing back further into the wall, Simion's eyes glare. "HELL NO! I ain't touching that thing! Watch out for the other one outside!"

Andrei quickly swivels the rifle. "Where! Other bear?" He steps around the bear to look out the door.

Simion points hesitantly up the ramp. "I saw." He restarts, trying to lower his very high-pitched voice, "I saw a smaller one up there around the corner. Make sure it doesn't come down." He clears his dry throat without moving his wide eyes off the doorway. Then, glancing down at his left arm, Simion notices that the sleeve is ripped and is slowly being discoloured. "Shit.

Must have got me." He holds his left arm up against his belly.

The gale is now clearing to the point where some of the tundra beyond the ramp can be picked out in the arctic noon. Simion notices a clump of flesh on the ground just outside the door. He is about to point it out to Andrei when a plaintive yelp comes again from the cub, hiding around the corner of the ramp wall. Hearing it, Andrei points his rifle up the ramp and lets off a shot, startling Simion.

"JESUS FRIGGEN CHRIST! What're you doing!"

Andrei smiles, then breaks into giggles, looking at Simion then outside and back again. "Simion! You want I should ask next time to shoot at bear?"

He starts laughing uncontrollably. Simion joins him, still holding his left arm. Their manic laughter echoes up the ramp.

Outside, the cub yelps again then backs away. He turns and runs. Stops, half turning back, then runs away over an embankment.

Unbonding

The Chovek house has old Western Star and Kenworth truck models and symbols on shelves, vying for space with family photos, curling pictures, blown-glass knick-knacks, along with small ceramic airplanes.

One picture shows a beaming Mr. Chovek holding a quiet infant, Damian, with his wife Sonja smiling next to them, all standing in front of a red biplane. Their older son, Mark, is peering up from the cockpit. The higher wing's shadow is over Sonja and half over Damian, splitting the picture into two distinct shades of contrast.

Sitting at the far end of a long kitchen table, Joe Chovek's face – considerably older and sadder than his picture – is wrinkled in concentration. He is in his forties, dressed in well-used casuals with streaks of grease and translucent finger blots of dried glue.

At the other end of the table, Sonja is a haggard forty-three-going-on-sixty. She has on a full apron that is splattered with multi-colored food stains. Her graying hair is unraveling wildly from a tie-back. Her cheeks and eyes have bits of oatmeal drying over reddened wrinkles.

Damian, their young autistic son, is wearing a dirty bib. He flails blindly at every move that his mother makes.

Chovek is reading a thin, green-bound report that is titled, *Annual Report, Chovek Truck Centre.*

He roughly marks a section with a big circle.

"Missed this, Murty! Used sales cost of goods sold is applied to Service!"

He shakes his head angrily.

A splat of oatmeal hits the report. A wild groan emanates from Damian, who is fighting off his mother's spoon.

Chovek stares with disgust at the splat. "Ah for chrissake!" He wipes off the oatmeal, awkwardly holding up his finger with the glob on it. He avoids looking at his wife.

Sonja is getting flailed by Damian. She persists in feeding him small spoons-full of oatmeal, grimly smiling while protecting her face from Damian's swinging arms.

The mess is overflowing into the living room. Her quiet tears mix with the oatmeal.

Damian emits a wild, "NOOOO!"

Still holding the one finger up, Chovek uses his free hand to toss the report roughly at a dark leather couch in the livingroom.

"I'm going out to the garage, Sonja!"

Sonja, distracted, mumbles, "What?"

"I'M GOING OUT TO THE GARAGE!"

She spares a glance from the battlefield at her departing husband, then turns her attention back to feeding Damian.

As the door closes behind Chovek, the garage becomes a dark zone of silence.

Chovek stands in the dark for a minute with his head down. He tries to think of better times, before they had... children.

He remembers when they were both younger, living in their first apartment. The memory clarifies. In their old dining room, Chovek is seated sideways playing a classical piece on a guitar, in shorts and tousled hair, leaning his scrubby chin over the guitar with a blank expression, expertly picking through the complicated notes.

A younger and prettier Sonja, dressed in a silk gown, is bringing him a plate of perfectly sequestered eggs.

He stares at the cooling eggs as she places it with both hands precisely in front of him.

He leans the guitar against another chair.

"Sonja, honey..."

"Yes, dear?"

"I'm very fragile this morning. I was wondering if..."

He shakes his head. "Oh never mind."

Still blank faced, he gets up with the plate and takes it into the kitchen.

BEEPS from a microwave can be heard.

Sonja sits stiffly, one fist flexing and unflexing.

Coldly, "Honey? What are you doing? Don't you like the eggs?"

A radio news broadcaster can just be heard from the living room.

Sonja gets up sharply and goes into the living room. The broadcaster can be heard saying, "…surprise lift off from the Peruvian plateau that has stunned world leaders. Reporting from Lima is Darrel McAlister…"

Chovek's head pops around the kitchen doorway.

An "off" click can be heard from the living room.

"Sonja. Can you turn that up, please?"

She comes back into the dining room and again sits stiffly at her place.

"Never mind the radio, Joe. I want to hear what you don't like about the way I make eggs."

Chovek jumps for the living room radio. He angrily punches it back on, then slowly backs into a chair, listening to McAlister.

"…apparently purchased from the Russians, which the group shipped to a port northwest of Lima, on a remote part of coastal Peru. In the meantime, over twelve hundred members of the group were secretly building their spaceport..."

The microwave dings.

"Joe. Whatever you were burning in the microwave is ready."

Frustrated, "Shushsh! I'm listening!"

"Well, there's no need to get hostile... And I'm still waiting for an explanation."

McAlister carries on, "...will report more fully on this remarkable situation when we reach the spaceport. This is Darrel McAlister reporting from Lima, Peru."

Chovek stiffens. "Shit! It's over!

He leans across to slam a finger into the radio's power button.

Staring angrily at the carpet at his feet, Chovek seethes.

"Sonja, for chrissake! Couldn't you see I was trying to hear something that was important?"

She gets up, hands on hips. "And what am I? Not important?

Sonja straightens to her full height of almost five feet.

"I was trying to find out why you took the eggs I prepared for you and threw them into the microwave!"

Still seated with his head down, Chovek is unrepentant, but tries to be reasonable. "You are important, Sonja. But what they were saying on the radio was..." He looks at her. "well – we could've had this conversation after the news and then I could've heard it."

Keeping her advantage, Sonja presses on. "Honestly! I don't know what's got into you, recently!" She faces him with arms crossed as he walks back into the kitchen. "Joe. Are you seeing someone else?"

Chovek straightens up in surprise, towering over her. "Huh? What're you talking about?"

His anger rising, he shakes his head.

"I get cold eggs, so I go and heat them up and then I want to hear news that'll probably change civilization on Earth, but you want to make up some cockamamie story about me seeing someone else?!

"Well maybe I bloody well should, if that's the way you're going to be!"

Shocked at what just happened, Sonja stands stock still for an instant, then slowly covers her mouth with her hands. She rushes out, then slams the door to the bedroom behind her.

Crying can be heard from inside.

Chovek looks at the bedroom door.

Quietly, "Go to hell. I'm not falling for that shit."

Chovek's flashback ends, leaving him with a solid shiver. "Well. Still together. Despite it all... And L5 is being built. Despite it all."

Letting out a sigh, he flicks on the garage lights. His eyes look haunted. Tears follow the lines in his cheeks, blurring his view. He wipes his eyes, twice.

In the glaring light before him, a twenty-foot-long plywood table holds wooden jigs, around which a lustrous ivory-colored wooden airplane fuselage is forming.

Next to it, a similar long table holds the right-side wing of his nascent airplane. Bright fresh wood almost shimmers in anticipation of flight.

Another wild groan from his son in the kitchen shakes Chovek again.

Remembering the oatmeal on his finger, he wipes it with a rag that he gets from his workbench. Half dried, it takes several rubs to get the sticky mess off. Then he finds some oatmeal on his eyebrow, which takes vigorous rubbing to remove.

Finally feeling clean, Chovek replaces the rag on a nail over the bench and sits on an old bar-stool. Without looking, his hand reaches to a panel of switches on one side of the bench, where it gives a flick of a remote switch to get the radio on. Beethoven's *À Thérèse* begins to play softly.

Turning on the stool, Chovek goes to the almost finished wing. He fondly caresses the new wood, inspecting the wing's interior.

Mumbling, "Inside needs a final sanding. Do that on the driveway. Nice day."

He goes to the big door, unlocks it at three places – dusting off a cobweb as he lifts a slide-lock – and opens the garage to happy sunlight.

Next door, his neighbour is trimming their mutual hedge. They wave at each other.

Chovek steps back inside to release the chocks at each of the wing-table's casters, then carefully maneuvers the table outside to the driveway.

Chovek wheels the table a few feet past the garage door where he locks the front casters.

The neighbour, Allen, comes over, shears in hand.

"Hey, Joe! What'cha got there?"

With a leery glance at the shears, "Morning, Allen. It's one of my wings. For that airplane I told you about."

A muffled wild yell comes from the house. They both hear it then resume their conversation.

"It doesn't look like it's gonna be done any time soon, there Joe."

He runs his fingers not-so-gently over the leading edge. Chovek stiffens as the shears get close to his prized wood.

"Oh sure. I could get it done this year, if, if..."

Allen holds his head down, peeking through an eyebrow.

"Listen. Joe?"

Chovek is occupied in locking the rear casters of the table.

"Yes?"

Allen eases into a request. "You know how you said, ah, a while ago, Joe, that, like..."

Chovek cringes as Allen absently waves his garden shears very close to his wing's perfectly sanded leading edge. He uses deliberate calm to avoid any sudden movement, placing his hand with a smooth motion to be between the shears and his prized wing.

"Ah, Allen, watch the wing, there."

Allen starts, "Huh? Oh! Yeah, shit, sorry Joe!"

He steps back a bit. Then moves forward again.

"Listen, I was wondering if I could borrow a few tools next weekend. Vera wants me to, ah, do a few things in the kitchen."

He tries to judge how that was received. Chovek is looking blankly at the lovely, rounded wing leading edge.

"You're the only guy around here who's got, like, a full wood shop and I was wondering, if you won't be doing anything in particular next weekend you could, like, bring over a few tools and help me take down those old cupboards."

He gauges Chovek again.

"And put up, help me put up some new ones."

Chovek catches on. "Just bring a few tools over and re-do your whole friggen kitchen next weekend? Is that all? Maybe we should do the floor too?"

A wry smile from Allen.

"Ah, well, might have to leave the floor for another week. What do you say, ol' buddy? I'd really appreciate it and it'd be a good diversion for you."

Allen gives a short nod back to Chovek's house.

Chovek shakes his head.

"What the hell. Sure. Got nothing better booked."

Allen grins and pats Chovek's shoulder.

Chovek nods at his wing.

"She's gonna be a real dilly, Allen. Can't wait to fly her. Why…"

Allen cuts in, "Listen, Joe. You sure this thing is gonna be strong enough to hold a guy in heavy winds? Like, it's just wood…"

"Strong enough?! This design's been around for years, Allen. No problems at all. It'll carry two people and some baggage. She's stressed for 8 Gs positive and 4 negative. I used only the best wood. It takes Sitka spruce for the spars and the ribs, and then it gets covered with high quality aircraft-grade one-eighth Birch plywood. I'll probably cover it next week." He grins wryly, "Or the week after."

Chovek proudly runs his hand over the finished, perfectly smooth, D-section leading edge. The interior of the wing, showing the spars and ribs, shines with the ivory white of expensive wood.

"The guy that designed it used to work for a French aircraft company. He was an aeronautical engineer and he came over to help out at the... well. I'm not supposed to say – or know – but he was working in the Lougheed Skunkworks."

Allen is unimpressed.

Chovek presses on, "You know!? They designed the spyplanes - the U2 and the Blackbird?"

Hesitantly, "Oh! *The Skunkworks...*"

Smiling, Chovek carries on, "Right! He knows what he's doing! This wing is extremely strong, because of the special materials used and the design. It has to take all kinds of loads, in tension and compression, plus torsion, 'cause the wing going through the air wants to twist up and away."

He holds out his hand, palm down, then slowly twists his palm and moves it up and back.

"Especially at the speed it's gonna go at. When you bomb along the highway at fifty miles-an-hour, I'm just taking off at that speed, and then I keep going to over a hundred! Downhill, or with a bigger engine, it can do almost two hundred!"

Now impressed, Allen is looking for a chink.

"Must be expensive. Even to build one yourself."

Chovek smiles broadly, "Well, it can be. Some of those fibreglass machines are well over a hundred thou'. But if you know what you're doing, get some good deals on stuff, well, I figure this one's only gonna cost about twenty-five thousand. Including the engine.

"I got a bunch of good deals at Oshkosh. That's an annual get-together that we have in Wisconsin. About a million people show up, and over twenty thousand airplanes of all kinds. They have what they call a Fly Market, where lots of people bring their stuff to sell."

He hitches a thumb back at the garage.

"Last year I picked up some instruments with glow-in-the-dark numbers and the special glue that's used for this wood. You have to coat one side with one part of the glue and then the other side with the other glue part – sort of a..." he leers and winks at Allen, "male-female thing. When you put 'em together and clamp 'em tight overnight, she sets up solid. I got a real deal on this bunch of glue 'cause it was older than they want to use for the factory jobs."

Allen touches the wing's leading edge again. "It was old glue?"

Chovek looks up at the clouds as he answers, "Well, yeah, but they have very tight regs for factory machines. We don't have to worry about the same set of regs for homebuilts."

Still not convinced, Allen turns away from the wing. "Yeah. Ok. But you're not gonna catch me off the ground in one of these things!"

"Oh come on, Allen! These machines are so well designed that," Chovek prepares to demonstrate by raising a stiff palm above the main spar.

"They're as solid as a rock!"

As he slams down on the spar, the wing ribs fall off the spar into their constituent pieces, rattling off the table and onto the driveway.

The pieces keep dribbling down.

Chovek's hand stays extended over the former wing for a minute.

His face turns as white as the ivory wood.

Allen walks away shaking his head, muttering. He snaps his shears twice.

"There's angels and there's idiots. I'm really not sure about you, Joe..." He mumbles to himself as he gets to his yard, "What's he trying to get a away from?"

THE FUTURE OF THE FUTURE

A recent meta-study has determined conclusively that the concept called "the Arrow of Time" (tAoT) has been based, at least partially, on calculations that were not entirely correct. The paper, called "The Prevention of Entropy by the Second Law of Thermodynamics and the Concomitant Negative Display of T-symmetry within Macroscopic Processes", was written by a group of mathematicians at the University of Victoria as a key component of their calculations to determine the future year-by-year trajectory of prices for condominiums and single-family homes in their local market area.

When a literature review was conducted by those researchers, they determined that calculations to support the principle of tAoT were not consistent with current research in thermodynamics. The principle calculations that had been relied on were by Carnot (1824), Clapeyron (1832), and Clausius (1854). The paper, pointedly, did not elaborate on Maxwell's famous thought experiment regarding a daemon who guarded two vessels of different temperature, mediating which molecules were to pass from one to the other. The researchers stated that their literature review and recalculations were confined to experiential factors. They did note that the further principle of the conservation of information may be at risk.

When the research was presented by the team lead, Viktor Mozhebite, at a conference in Banff, Alberta, at least one of the attendees objected vociferously. After extensive conversations, the objecting physicist, Mehak Singh Ucisora, did agree to perform the calculations independently.

Using the 3g quantum computer at her university in North Carolina, the physicist reported that she could not disprove the original paper's main hypothesis.

Therefore, the two agreed to prepare a paper for publication, focusing on the discrepancy in the subject calculations. In the expectation that such a paper would not be well received by either the standard journals or through peer review, they offered their paper to an obscure astrophysics journal, the Proceedings on Submolecular Astrophysics (PSA).

The subsequent storm of controversy has been termed in the general scientific press as the William Tell Black Hole (WTBH).

When contacted by this reporter, the editor of the journal would not directly confirm that the original acronym was from the words "What The Bloody Hell?"

Implications

The concept of the Arrow of Time presumes that all events at the macroscopic level proceed inevitably to entropy, or chaos. An increase in entropy, and the concomitant decrease in order of a system, can be visualized as sand castles on a beach. Intuitively, one would not expect to see sand castles being built up spontaneously on a beach. Rather, as waves get pushed further ashore, any castle succumbs to their inevitable washing action, flattening the castle. To see the castles build up after a series of waves, forming higher and cleaner structures, would be illogical. With the findings in this paper, it may be that such phenomena may yet be seen.

As the Arrow of Time is an analogy of the march toward the future, one is left to speculate on the *inevitability* of a step-by-step march toward a "future". Is there a track, off which we cannot step? Is there a velocity associated with the trajectory? How many Arrows are there? Is the viewer of their own Arrow *obligated* to move toward a particular direction? Are all Arrows following the same direction? At the same velocity?

Might one step backwards? Or sideways?

Or down?

LOVE IS WAR

Company cubicles, coming up to lunchtime.

Roselyn (Rosey), is a twenty-two year old woman dressed in a fashionable short dress and tight sweater. Her colour choices today reflect the bright sunny days that have taken over for the summer. Her cubicle has some pictures of the current young male movie star heart-throbs. From a distance, we see that Elena, with a similarly coloured shirt though in black yoga pants, comes and chats.

Still conversing, Rosey finishes typing and gets up. She takes her purse, confirming that her phone is inside. She and Elena head down the hall, close enough that they rub arms several times. With their outside arms, they both check for updates on their phones as they walk almost arm-in-arm toward the elevator. They are good friends.

But first they hit the washroom together.

Company cafeteria.

The cafeteria is loud with a hundred conversations. Pennants proclaim the monthly theme: South America.

Smells of spicy dishes waft around the room. People flow slowly along the hot-foods line then disperse quickly around the large, airy room.

Rosey and Elena talk while in the food line. Rosey hears a ding from her phone and opens it to see the notification. Quickly, she appears to look away, examining closely one of the food items, in the process moving her phone away from Elena's view. She closes her phone without further action.

Elena notices the move. "Who's that, your secret lover?" Her smile is anticipatory.

Rosey wants to shrug it off then offers a wry grin. "El, honey, it's just a missile from Kenney, your current flame. He wants to do us both under the totems in Stanley Park."

"HUH!" Elena snorts loudly enough to make heads turn. "If that dim-witted nerd ever had a sensuous thought in his linear mind, it'd melt the contents of his bald head down his double throat!"

Nearby people in the line smile but keep their attention on the food options and the upcoming server at the counter.

"So why do you still have coffee with him?"

"Good question. 'Cause he pays for my lattes?... Naw. 'Cause he'd probably go postal if I dumped him? Maybe... How do we get ourselves *into* this shit?" Elena shakes her head.

Rosey is satisfied that she has distracted her friend.

Taking their orders on trays, the two divide their attention between looking for an open table and checking out who is sitting with whom. Rosey sees Elena's bald supervisor wink at her as he holds his phone suggestively. She automatically steers the other way, bumping Elena's tray.

"Hey! Take it easy, Rosey. You see someone over here?"

Deliberately walking away from the winker, "No. I remember I get a cold draft from the main entrance area. Oh! Isn't that Shannon with the new-hire from IT? Why don't we go over to play cupid? Or something?" They both giggle as they weave their way to Shannon's table.

Elena gets there first and stands beside the IT guy. She notices his couple days of facial hair growth. "Hey Shannon! You're looking particularly glowing today."

She winks at the IT guy, who blushes and puts his head down, chin nuzzling against his white golf-shirt.

Rosey takes up a flanking position. "Ohh, I love that pink sweater, don't you Elena? The frills add just the right touch. And I don't think it quite exceeds his royal arseness' rules for exposure."

The IT guy perks his head up, briefly taking in a full view of Elena's fulsome breasts a few inches from his head, "Royal Arseness?"

Shannon feels she must rein in her friends with a few words of her own. "Oh, they're making fun of the department manager. You know him, Billy? And, by the way, these two lovely gossips are Elena and Rosey." She nods at each in turn while an embarrassed Billy almost raises his eyes enough to acknowledge them. "Billy is our new expert in Security App Installations and Troubleshooting."

Rosey grins down at Billy, "SAIP?"

A smile and another extended perusal of Elena's best, "Yeah. Better than Password Parsing and Totalizing." He continues to smile at all three for a minute until it becomes clear they do not get his joke.

Elena takes a stab, "PPT?"

"No no. Passpartoot. Get it?"

Rolled eyes all around.

"Shannon, honey, you've got your work cut out for you." Rosey gives Shannon the eye and steers Elena to an open table nearby.

Elena glances back over her shoulder at Billy, who is following her with his eyes. Elena tosses her mostly blonde hair. Billy gets a jab in the ribs from Shannon's sharp elbow.

Company cubicles, next morning.

Billy enters the office area shyly. He is now clean shaven and wearing a medium blue button-up shirt and grey dress-slacks. He is carrying a small briefcase.

Elena happens to look in his direction and holds her gaze on him for a while, confirming it really is the same scruffy-looking Billy she saw in the cafeteria. He sees her and makes a bee-line for her desk, negotiating the obstacle course of low dividers and plants.

Rosey notices Billy's trajectory. A smile forms as she sees the deliberateness of his approach. Still working, she continues to track Billy, and Elena's reaction, with interest.

Billy arrives at his target. "Hi. Ah… I, ah, I'm doing a security audit. Just a random audit. And, ah, I was wondering if you have a few minutes?"

"Oh, hi Billy. Well, like, ok. If you can give me a minute so's I can finish this off?" She nods at a spreadsheet on her screen.

Nodding eagerly, too quickly, "Sure. Yeah, that's fine. I'll just, ah, wait… "

Cafeteria, same day.

Shannon is sitting with Billy. She has on another fetching blouse that might well exceed his royal arseness' specification for skin exposure. Billy is distracted, not listening attentively to Shannon's opinion on the outlandish cost of rentals in the city.

"Billy! I asked what you think. I hate it when you just mumble 'Um' at everything I say!" She is annoyed with his wandering eyes today. "Are you ok?" She leans toward him, opening up her cleavage more suggestively. "You have something on your mind?"

When a slight jiggle doesn't capture his attention she leans back and combs a hand through her hair.

Billy continues to scan the arriving workers. As Elena and Rosey enter the cafeteria he sits up.

Shannon sees the object of his focused attention. "Elena and Rosey. Is that who you're looking for? Billy?"

"Ah, yeah. I, ah, had to do a security audit this morning on, on Elena's computer. Wanted to see if it's still working ok."

Shannon gives a perfunctory wave at Rosey. The line moves quickly and Rosey and Elena make their way directly to Shannon's table. Elena takes the chair next to Billy as Rosey and Shannon pass pleasantries.

Billy puts his nose down and munches loudly through his salad. After a minute his throat gets a message through to his brain regarding the excessive heat of the jalapeño peppers. "OW! AH ah water!"

There is no water but Elena gives him her orange juice. He grabs it and guzzles it desperately, as Rosey is trying to say, "You really shouldn't. Water makes it worse…"

Billy's face turns a bright red as he struggles to breathe between gulps.

Shannon sits back. "Serves you right for inhaling your food like that… Are you alright, Billy?"

Rosey breaks off some of her bread and offers it to him. Billy takes it in one gulp.

Rosey still holds her fingers out after his grab. "You should let the bread absorb…"

He swallows it whole. He starts to cough and choke. After an ineffectual cough, with his face changing from red toward blue, Elena slaps his back, then again, harder. Billy coughs more productively, spraying wet bits around the table.

Shannon recoils, pulling her hands away from the table, "Oo! Yuck. Billy!"

Rosey wipes a few pieces from her shirt then starts to clean up the table as Billy has more controlled coughs. "Well, never mind that. Clean-up in aisle three. I guess we're not finishing lunch today." Concerned with Billy, "Are you ok now?"

Billy nods sheepishly, wipes his mouth, then has a couple more clearing coughs. Elena has been holding him by his shoulders, with a worried, motherly look.

Leaning forward, Shannon has noticed the support that Elena is giving him. She stands up and takes his hand. "Come on honey. Let me take you to the washroom. We both need to clean up." She flashes an angry glance at Elena. "If Elena hadn't stuffed that bread down your throat you'd be alright."

Elena is blindsided, "Huh? I didn't…"

Shannon shuffles Billy away.

Elena looks for support from Rosey, pleading, "I didn't give him the bread."

"Of course not. I did. It wasn't the bread. It was the double dose of jalapeños. Don't sweat it, El. Shannon is like that."

"Well, why'd she accuse me…?"

"Listen, El. You were getting too close to her prize. You know that Billy's family owns property in the west end?"

"Huh? What's that got to do…?"

"Come on, kid. He was panting for you like a puppy. What do you expect her to do?"

"Like, besides not yelling at him for getting sick with those peppers? Poor guy. Didn't think she was like that."

Company cubicles, next morning.

Office noises – one-sided conversations with clients on the phone, chairs creaking – all under the bright lights of too many fluorescents and creeping bands of sunlight from wide windows.

Rosey stretches up from her chair and decides to take her mid-morning break. Elena joins her in the can.

As Rosey is washing her hands, Elena is in front of the mirror. This surprises Rosey.

"War paint?"

"What?"

"You usually leave that for the weekend battles."

Elena is now self-conscious. She corrects a smudge with more powder on her left cheek. "Just... you know, being a little more presentable... Is it too much?"

"Don't ask me, El. I'm not the target."

"Huh? What do you mean?" Elena is getting agitated.

Not wanting to put Elena into a bad mood, "You look lovely, El. You really do."

Elena calms down, checking her profile in the mirror.

It elicits a smile from Rosey. "Billy coming to do another security check?"

Elena stops, collects her accessories into her purse and asks testily, "So what if he is?"

"Nothing at all, dear. Nothing at all."

As Elena turns to leave, Rosey can't help mumbling, "May the best woman win."

Bistro, that weekend.

Loud music, yelling conversations, lights flashing, gyrating dancers on the floor, small groups and twosomes more-or-less conversing at tables and on couches around the dance floor. Some are drinking, some are taking other forms of mind-altering chemicals. Much smiling and nodding.

Elena is dressed in a knock-out bright tangerine and neon blue combo that mostly contains her ample figure. Rosey is, in her own way, more subtly attractive in a light green and tan dress. They are both wearing high heels, though Elena's look weaponized.

Occupying a white leather couch, their drinks are on a low table in front. An already empty glass sits behind Elena's current drink. Elena is being unusually flamboyant with her arm gestures, attracting many appreciative glances and stares from nearby male dancers.

Shannon comes arm-in-arm with Billy as she leads him into the room. Her outfit is bright, tight and revealing but she is on edge. Billy is not at all comfortable in this environment. His yellow golf shirt and light grey slacks might have been appropriate a generation ago. He looks around for a corner to hide in.

The crowd is more dense in front of Elena, so she does not notice Billy right away. Her sensors, however, are in high tension so when she does glimpse Billy, Elena rises immediately. Bending back down to speak to Rosey, she has to hold her breasts under cover. Yelling, with a bit of a slur, "I'm going to resupply. Want another one yet?"

Shaking her head, Rosey shows her half-full glass. Elena downs her own drink with a glug and heads for where she last saw Billy.

Meanwhile, Shannon's defensive antennas are in tune. She has detected the gathered crowd, presumed to be around Elena, and instinctively steers Billy to the far side of the bar area.

Getting the attention of a bartender, she yells, "Two red wines, please. Large glasses."

As Shannon pays for the drinks, she is dismayed to discover that Elena is already zeroing in on Billy. Elena's approach takes her, rather aggressively, through the dancers. One of the guys objects to Elena's drunken bump and turns to yell at her. She bats her eyelashes and deflects his anger with an air kiss and a forward lean. Elena swings unsteadily past the now-smiling dancer to resume her attack.

Meanwhile, Shannon has moved with Billy into a defensive position behind a couch. She places Billy with his back to a large light fixture that blocks the path to the other end of the couch, then pats the top cushion for Billy to sit on. She smiles down to greet the couch's mostly-oblivious occupants. The wall, a meter and a half behind the couch, is mirrored so it affords good 360° visibility.

As Elena comes up to the couch, Shannon ignores her and continues to keep Billy occupied with random yelled questions.

He is being overwhelmed by the mass of datapoints hitting every sensor. All he sees is Shannon's flapping mouth. Billy falls into a panic attack and pushes past Shannon, through the dancers. He bumps into the previously bumped dancer who yells at him. Billy starts to put his hands up to his ears to shut the world out but receives a quick uppercut from the angry dancer. A nearby dancer, seeing the unfairness of the attack, tries to get between Billy and his attacker. The Good Samaritan has to duck another swing from the now enraged attacker, who believes a group is after him. Meanwhile, Billy is on the floor, crawling away desperately from the developing brawl.

Back at the couch, Shannon takes the opportunity to blindside a distracted Elena, sending her down onto the couch occupiers. Rosey sees the punch and hurries over to her friend, narrowly avoiding the shoving dancers. Getting to a woozy Elena, who is being petted in various parts of her body by the four people she landed on, Rosey starts yelling at Shannon just as the music is turned off. "YOU" music off "BITCH!" Quieter, "You took a swing at her when she wasn't looking! What's got into you?"

The ambient noise, devoid of booming speakers, gets louder as everyone starts yelling at each other: encouraging the fights to go on, commenting on the action, and, from a few plaintive voices, "Will you all please just calm down?"

Someone turns the lights on to a dazzling brightness. Lasers no longer flash. The uncomfortable exposure suddenly stops most of the battles. People begin to exit the arena, then the dribble becomes a push for the exit.

The crowd erupts onto the street, lit only by orange streetlights, prompting a few to carry on the grudges they had developed in the bistro.

Company cubicles, Monday.

Elena arrives off the elevator to start her day with a smile. Already there, Rosey greets her cautiously with a whisper.

"El, that bruise is fully covered up. Just saying. Your kiddy grin might start to wrinkle the makeup, though."

"Yes, a lovely day, isn't it? And how are you doing this fine Monday morning, Rosey?"

"Elena? Is that you?" Rosey takes Elena's hands to hold her down from floating up to cloud nine.

"Don't be silly, Rosey. I didn't put that much makeup on, did I?" Suddenly concerned, she reaches for her makeup mirror.

"No no. I mean, like, you *hate* Mondays. Did Shannon give you a concussion or something?"

With a touch of bemusement, "Shannon? Shannon who?"

"Ok. So, do you remember Billy?"

Elena starts to melt into a sugary creampuff. "Oh, Billy's fine. Just fine." She focuses on Rosey, "He called me Sunday morning. He was so sweet. Wanted to apologize and all that so I said 'Let's do lunch and you can pay and tell me all about what happened last night'. He came out of his shell. Totally. He said all it takes to get him comfortable is to have lunch at the Sylvia. So we stayed and had supper, too. He talked forever. All about his parents, who he adores, and about sailing. Do you know what a baggywrinkle is?"

"Huh?"

Elena eyes the stars dreamily, "Billy says it's like a long mop-end that stops the chafing of a line next to a yard."

Stifling a laugh, "Gotta remember that if my jeans get too tight." Rosey looks up at the digital clock. "Off to work we go." She takes Elena's hand with some concern. "Listen, kid. I know you're in a zone, but this place is not that zone. Wake up, or his Nibs'll be standing over your desk. Ok?"

Still in dreamland, "Fine."

Bus Delivery

Mountains thrust rough crests grandly into and through
Cloudscapes of crystal mist feathered by high wind.

Snow paints long lines across masses of rock,
Jumping with purpose from crag to peak.

There, rocks flow through time, with jagged aprons down,
Becoming stones becoming soil becoming fertile food
And with flowing water and rushing wind, fall away into sea.

Misty waves stretch far beyond forested hills,
Rich sea holds green and coloured life in deep mysteries.

Creeping up from dripping wet cool shoreline,
Forest paints green/orange/yellow gowns
Against mountains that boldly hold up the sky.

Marching steadily upwards, stubby conifers dig deep
Into crumbling mountain slopes.
A rough rutted round rock road can be seen in slashes through
forest, then emerges
From enduring green shields clinging in life-grip against mountain.
Lush sharp pine branches waft resinous tones into playful air.

Rising sun burns through vertical, cold rising sea-borne mist.
Sun blazes omnipotent red and orange cloudscapes
Across horizon in bright splashes of colour
Over-laying lowland forest's pale carpet.

Bluejay sings out in joyful, melodious voice
On mountain's sunward slope.

Its voice changes to a harsh warning scream as a gaudy huffing vehicle bursts up from mountain's lush evergreens. Billowing gray smoke tinges trees ahead of the bus, challenging forest's resinous signature. Ravens wake each other around mountain's slope, and bluejay, overwhelming the sound of twittering squirrel and thrushes, is himself finally drowned out by the clattering diesel bus that growls up the gravel road.

Ground wind skitters in angry cold aimless circles, not knowing how to get away from the acrid fumes that lead the mechanical beast. Climbing up the road, the bus whines through lower and lower gears. It rattles to a stop in front of a stone and log house that stands half way up eastern slope.

Stone is piled up against the downslope side of the house, not for decoration, but to combat winter wind that usually batters hard at mountain.

The bus driver's weathered face peers through a hazy side window, looking for movement from the house. He jabs at the horn, sending a receding series of echoes down mountain's grey slopes. Circling eagle veers away on chilly high wind to find friendlier territory.

"Where the hell *are* they, for chrissake! My ticker..." He rubs his chest over a previous operation.

The driver pulls up the parking brake. Reaching for some of the meager heat being blasted out of the fans, he rubs his hands together. This uncovers his back, so he hunkers into the seat again.

He looks around to make sure everything appears alright. Spotting some chipped paint around the speedometer, he quickly rubs at the paint next to the chrome dial rim with a greasy finger and makes it look old and undisturbed again. He examines the odometer closely for any leftover scratches.

"Can't do a damn thing about it now, anyway," he mumbles, climbing out of the cracked vinyl seat.

Opening the door with a rush of escaping heated air, he yells out, "SAMMY! WHERE THE HELL ARE YOU!"

Then he quickly pulls back on the chrome door lever to quiet the suddenly roaring fans.

As the driver flops back onto his seat, his rear end feels ice cold again on the vinyl. He half-heartedly wiggles the heat control knobs, wishing he'd brought a blanket and to hell with appearances. A vigorous rub of his thighs doesn't help much, so he snuggles his head into his coat's brown furry collar and thrusts his hands into leather coat pockets, hunkering down for a cold wait. Damned if he is going out into that frigid air, even for a good sale.

Inside the dwelling, Sammy is arguing with his seventeen year old son. They are in the lower level of a log cabin. A blackened wood-stove hums its way through hardwood fuel. A smiling red glow wafts smaller and larger near the top of its firebox. Its black stove-pipe twists a few times before poking up through a wide, metal-sealed hole in the wood-plank ceiling. A square of roughly cut corrugated sheet, separating the pipe from the wall planks, pings every once-in-a-while as it gets cooled and then is reheated.

The young man is slouched deeply into a greyish straw-filled grain sack. A three-quarter length brown corduroy coat is pulled half-on over the youngster's left side, which is facing the outside wall.

His mind swims past old scenes.

He was eleven, in summer light clothes,
Racing up back meadow, over tufted grass,
Toward his favourite beech forest.
Boy jumps over granite boulders
That hold back the cow grass and smothering plops of cow dung.

Gliding with light summer wind
Over soft leaf-covered forest food,
Joyfully around great feeding beeches,
Carefully by springy, thin ten-foot shoots.
Boy stops under dour old spruce,
Home of squirrels
And birds

And ants crawling with purpose
Up and down rutted bark.
Fragrant spruce stands high beside old beech,
Fronds outstretched, welcoming warm sun.

"Will you please stop nodding and answer me!?"

Boy pads quietly but fast-as-wind
Through raspberry stocks and clumped grasses.
Long pants are grabbed by each stock,
Holding tight, leaving pulled threads...

"Sandy!"

Desperate to get back to summer, Sandy flings his head into the soft pillow, but Sammy whacks his bum so hard he jumps out of summer into the withering winter stare of his father.

"Sandy! What the hell's gotten into you? We have to go! The guy's out there waiting for us with our new Bus! Grab your bag! Come on!"

They finish getting dressed, then Sandy follows his father, reluctantly, out into the winter wind.

Sammy clomps along the rough gravel path from his house, down toward his new bus. He pulls his brown felt trench-coat collar tight against his neck. Holding a huge duffle bag awkwardly with bulging muscles, he shifts it to his other hand.

"Wanna just put these bags in and try the thing. Wanna see if it's the same Bus that we bought."

Sandy trudges behind, head down, holding his green duffle bag to his chest to help ward off the biting cold wind. He stumbles a bit, kicking a chunk of gravel past his father's leg.

> Distant eagle calls,
> Far, then farther away.
> Boy looks up, sees only high clouds
> Playing at shapes
> With feather strokes
> In four dimensions.

He nearly runs into the bus door. Sammy is bouncing up the stairs, holding out his hand to the driver, who gets up from the seat.

"Sammy Sullivan! Great to see you again! Come on in! Let your son in so we can close the door!"

"Jeremiah, how are you! Very happy to see you with my new Bus! She looks great! Doesn't she, Sandy?"

"Humph."

Sandy struggles by his father and takes a seat. It is rock hard and cold as a block of ice. He jumps up, leaving his bag, and goes in search of warmth next to a blasting heater about two-thirds of the way down the aisle.

Pulling his coat tightly around him, Sandy tries to warm the seat enough for it to soften a little under his bum. Sammy drops his bag on Sandy's on the front seat.

Sandy starts to shiver.

Wondering if it's any warmer up front, he pokes his head up a little from inside his collar to see his father and the driver. He decides it's too much trouble to move, so Sandy hunkers down into the seat, avoiding the metal wall to his right.

Sammy pushes the bags with his hip so he can sit down, as his arms overflow the metal barrier by the stairs. Two heaters are roaring away right at him. The bus smells unpleasantly of diesel and disinfectant. Whatever mint was in a swinging ornament on the windscreen by the door has been long lost, miles ago.

"So, Jeremiah. The Bus made it up the mountain! I really was wondering if the old diesel could do it! If she works out, there are folks on both sides of this mountain who'd like to have this connecting road made a lot busier! Can she do this climb twice a day?" Sammy looks Jeremiah's face over carefully for any reaction.

Poker-face smiles slightly. "Of course it can make it, Sammy! No doubt at all. Why, like I said, she's as good as brand new. Look at the mileage! You know that a diesel's gonna go a long way and for many, many years. This one's not even hitting 200 thou' yet. Like I said, Sammy, you got a real deal. This bus was only used for a local route, so's it ain't got the miles that a ten or nine year old bus might have. A real deal!"

Jeremiah can't help looking down at the odometer. He catches himself and changes the subject.

"Sammy, my friend; I'm gonna show you how to be a bus driver! Are you ready?"

He puts it into first gear, pulls the parking brake and roars forward. Normally he would have started in second, but he wants to show how much torque the old engine has. Smiling broadly as the bus sprints downhill, Jeremiah shows off its handling by weaving deftly around the potholes.

They drive back into the forest. As Jeremiah has been counting on, the downhill run needs more braking than engine work so the rough engine is not as obvious. Hairpin turns are the only times he has to run through the gears. Curiously, branches seem to reach out to slap the bus. They hit the outside mirrors several times, knocking them out of alignment and the roof gets a bumping scrape more than once. Jeremiah had not noticed any of those problems while driving up. He is confused.

Arriving at the edge of old forest Jeremiah cannot help slowing down to take in the view. Rough talus slope stretches to their right, and the narrow road seems to disappear downslope. As the bus slips and slides over the loose gravel, Jeremiah has trouble steering around newly fallen, sharp-edged rocks. The road becomes no more than a tight single lane so that he has to slow right down to bump over several of the large rocks while staying away from the edge and the long fall.

Eyes peeled to the road, "Must have been a rockfall since I drove up. The road was nothing like this…"

Just then Sandy catches a glimpse of something out of the corner of his eye. "Look out!"

A boulder smashes downslope and bounces once, flying directly onto the engine compartment. Jeremiah slams on the brake at the same time, sending Sammy into the windscreen.

Stopped with one front wheel hanging off the road, the bus engine grinds and stutters to a stop.

Sandy was thrown forward onto the back of the next seat. He clears his head as he stands up carefully. Hearing a moan from his father, he rushes forward along the aisle, reaching his staggering father. Sammy is bleeding from his forehead, the blood running over his face alarmingly.

Before Sandy can help, Sammy grabs for the door opener and, leaning on it, accidentally pulls the door open then stumbles down the steps. Sandy catches his other arm on the way down but they both fall outside. As they do so, the bus lurches forward toward the cliff edge.

Helping his father away from the bus wheel, onto the gravel, Sandy jumps back into the bus, trying to reach Jeremiah. As he gets the top step, the bus lurches ahead again throwing Sandy against the right-side seat. He lands on their two bags. Sandy takes the heavy top bag's handle, swinging it out the door. It lands on the last step then rolls off onto the gravel.

Wanting to help Jeremiah, Sandy reaches over to him. He sees a motionless body slumped over the steering wheel, blood dribbling from his mouth. Shaking Jeremiah's shoulder produces no response. The bus lurches forward again, then begins a slow grinding slide. Sandy grabs his bag from the front seat in one motion as he jumps for the steps. As he is pulling his trailing leg out of the bus the last step rises sharply, causing Sandy to lose his balance, flipping him into a heap beside his father. The bus disappears over the edge and grinds down the slope.

Overhead, eagle cries out as it circles the scene.

Sammy wipes some of the blood from his eyes with a hand, then with his sleeve. He sees the fresh trail of disturbed rocks where the bus had been and hears the crashing vehicle as it rolls to the river far below. "Oh my god!... Sandy!... Where's Jeremiah?"

He turns to his son, finding Sandy's arm and holding on tight.

Pulling himself into a sitting position, Sandy finds a few tissues in his coat pocket with his free hand. He gently wipes his father's face, removing some of the already drying blood. "Dad, I couldn't save him. He was... he wasn't moving and I didn't have time to pull him out. And..."

"My god, Sandy. Are you alright?"

Shaking his head slowly, Sandy starts to shiver. "It just rolled over the cliff."

They both embrace tightly, sitting on the gravel.

With his head on his father's shoulder Sandy mumbles, "Mountain really didn't want the bus up here." He pulls back a bit to speak to his father. "Promise me you won't bring another one up here, dad. Please?"

SQUIDS AND FREE WILL

The absolute quiet wakes Simion with a start. Not wanting to let the least bit of heat out of his sleeping bag, he moves very carefully to face the pingo's door. It looks OK.

The little ceramic heater is clicking its way toward cold.

He makes a minor but critical adjustment to a flap of blanket that covers the back of his head, up to his night toque.

Minutes, or tens of minutes, go by. Simion goes over in his mind what happened during the day; what he could have done better; what he wished he had been quicker about doing; the hot, monstrous mouth that was inches from his neck...

"This is going to be one of those long nights," he mumbles.

"Dah," answers Andrei.

"You awake too?"

"Heater wake me. Click, click, click. Never end. Get warm, get cold. You snore. Never end."

Smiling, "I try hard. Perhaps if I lay on my back I can manage to let out some formidable snorts for you... At least it could keep the animals away." Simion debates whether he should speak frankly. Something, anything to take his mind off that hot gaping mouth.

"Andrei."

"Still here, my friend."

Pensively, "Good… Do you ever wonder, ah, if people can hear, like, what…" He trails off.

"Like what what?"

"Things have happened to me, sometimes, so that I'm certain that, well, people can sometimes hear some of what I think."

Andrei tries to remember the word. "Telepathy."

"Yeah. Probably silly…"

"Know about squid?"

"Eight slithery tentacles; good camouflage; whales consider them a delicacy."

"Speak with colour. Every cell on skin can change colour and, and texture. When nearby squid look sexy, colour shimmers in pattern. When food come in big bunch, squid tells other squid with shades of colour. When you catch squid for table, turn red 'cause it mad as hell. Very smart – to control all of skin needs lots of neurons."

"I didn't know that, Andrei. I promise, the next time I have sushi, I'll give it some thought."

"What about colour-blind squid?"

"Huh?"

"What if one squid see no colour? Only grey. This squid see other squid talk and do thing, but colour-blind squid only see grey. Think other squid know what they say 'cause of telepathy. Must be something like telepathy, 'cause language of grey say little. Everybody must speak with telepathy, he think. He is wrong."

Simion is stunned by the analogy.

Andrei carries on, "Is like Asperger symptom."

"Ok. Ok, but I might have a little bit of that, yes, but why can people hear me?"

Andrei ponders that. "If true, prove. Think word. No – need science study…" He is about to launch into a research proposal.

"Thanks, Andrei, but never mind. I've already gone through that at a university. Did an intensive four hours of trying to beam my thoughts at research subjects. Nothing. Then, when the oh-so-skeptical assistant prof was wrapping up and telling me about random chance and probability, and I was so tired I just wanted to go and flake out on a couch, I was thinking, what the hell time is it? And he looks at his watch and says, 'Four o'clock.' I asked him why he said that. He said, 'Because you asked me.' I said, no I didn't. The argument went on for a while, but nothing good came of it. So I've never brought it up before…"

Now, Andrei is wide awake. He tries to make a conscious effort to not think – which, of course, entails strenuous thinking. Soon he slips back to sleep, exhausted.

Simion ponders the Aspergers analogy. He thinks that it explains a few things… Sleep.

Next morning, Simion is still thinking about the colour-blind squid. He puts it into a letter to Laura. His and Andrei's letters are saved in a mail packet.

By the time the next community supply plane from Inuvik comes through a week later, Simion adds a postcard to her in the packet.

Via the same plane, Mikey Qoppik gets a very short letter from his new southern friend. Picking the letter up at the grocer/post office, he expects it to be his instructions about the southern bastards. Reading it outside the store, its short threat and simple demand makes him physically sick. Stumbling down an alley, he retches against a building.

Collecting himself, he pulls the crumpled, unsigned note from his pocket and holds it at arm's length, as if it were contaminated. The message doesn't change: *The money has been deposited in your paypal account. You are now committed. Kill them. Or I kill you and your parents.*

Another listless night for Simion in the pingo. It is warmer, so he rolls over with less care about his blanket.

"*Warmer! What's wrong?*" he thinks, sitting up with a start. "*The amount of light bleeding in around the door looks ok . Andrei is… breathing ok . Did the weather change?*"

Listening intently, he hears nothing out of the ordinary. He settles back down, causing the plywood under his sleeping bag to creak against the gravel.

Andrei's head turns toward him slowly. "Shto?"

"Nothing. Too warm. It woke me."

Now Andrei does a perimeter search with his head raised. "Ok?"

"Yeah, I think so. Must be warmer outside."

"Dah." He rolls to his other side.

Several minutes pass.

"You're not sleeping, are you?"

"No, my friend. Adrenalin do good job to keep head spinning. Thank you."

Pause. He carries on, "Jebem. What is? Smell wood cell burning."

"Grey cells. Just… thinking."

"About…"

Simion sniffs. "About, well, I have this funny way of thinking." He cuts off Andrei's retort, "Yeah, and you're crazy too, but it's like…"

"Like vodka fog?"

"Shiraz is better for you. No. You know, I have this feeling/idea/certainty someplace in the back of my mind that if I can only take time to drag it out from back there, that there's something that'll be really important… That it'll be an important contribution to how we see our society in the context of why we're here." He started slowly but ends with real feeling.

Andrei's mind is thrown into visions of Paluntov saying the same thing, then he frantically races his mind in a dozen directions at once to avoid what he imagines is "transmitting". Outwardly, Andrei is tensely stiff, focusing on a sliver of light from the door.

The lack of a voiced reply makes Simion think Andrei is ignoring him.

"Andrei! This is important!"

He relaxes a bit. "Three times important. Good job. Thank you – you make me sleep now." He produces a snore, wide awake, still on the defensive.

A minute passes.

The effort is exhausting. Andrei rolls to his other side to calm down. He uses Simion's technique of tossing out a non sequitur. "At night, I wake up sometime and think, 'Bozhe moi! Is brilliant idea! Have to write idea down! Do in dark. In morning, words and scribble make no sense. Think grand idea in sleep. In morning light is all mish-mush. Mean nothing. Just nice dream… Go to sleep. Have more nice dream."

Simion shakes his head. "Something weird is going on, Andrei. It's not like I can hear voices in my head…"

Nodding, "Is good."

"It's that I find myself – I don't know how; mostly when I'm tired – I'm actually inside somebody's mind…"

Renewed panic scrambles Andrei's thoughts. Simion waves at a buzzing sound around his ears.

"Is dangerous. Very dangerous, my friend." Andrei sits up awkwardly, focusing on the outline of light around the door. He pulls his legs from out of the sleeping bag and sits on the box next to his bed.

Suddenly Simion feels a hot panic that he hadn't felt since the three bullies from the block near his house caught him in an alley contemplating a twenty-dollar bill he'd found outside the local pub.

Heart racing, "What... what do you mean dangerous? Andrei?" Unwelcomed words push forward in his mind: *cold death-trap, Russian soldier, rifle, middle-of-friggen-nowhere.* He fumbles franticly with his sleeping bag, getting the extra blanket caught around his good arm.

Andrei turns toward him. Quietly, "Stop."

Simion finally extracts himself, standing and breathing heavily on his side of the beds.

Staring back at the door, Andrei pulls out thoughts he never knew he had.

"Do not know if you hear me in ears or head. No matter – in pingo, in Mofin, attack by bear, we are friend, always."

He turns again to face Simion. "Have poor English. But need to tell important thing. Man from Oceanographic Institute, Director Paluntov, very smart. More smart than anybody I know. He study philosophy, like you. He know much more." Andrei smiles kindly at Simion. "Maybe you learn more in future."

Simion is about to say something but Andrei holds up a hand.

"Paluntov tell me this philosophy very hard for understand. When he say this, I think he joke. Is impossible for simple Andrei to understand. Can say this. Philosophy guys always try understand what means person and what means community. And what connection is."

Simion lights up. This is his favourite topic, with which he has turned many a party into stone.

"Ok. Like the presocratics, and then Sophists…"

"Only Sophis I know is last name Loren."

Completely undeterred, Simion catches fire. "So the Greeks started the *rational* movement by questioning what an individual could do to change the course that their fickle gods had put him on. They came up with the idea that free will was something separate from the will of the gods or even the will of the community. And that it must be some *thing* that went along with your body but wasn't really part of your body."

"Paluntov have same eye like you. See thing not there." Andrei, at this point, dearly wants to be speak and understand these concepts with Paluntov in

Russian. He wants to engage intellectually with Simion, and yet the language barrier is palpable.

"The monotheistic religions…"

Andrei jumps in, "Tradition guys. Close-mind tradition…"

"Ok ok. You're right. It was the traditionalists in the main religions that always took power away from the thinkers." Simion shakes his head. "Why do we always end up getting led by closed-minded, as you say, power-hungry people with only enough vision to stay in control! Self-appointed gatekeepers!"

"You read this? My, my teacher say…"

When Simion is excited about a topic he forgets to be respectful of the other's opinion. "I took this in university. Philosophy, religion, anthropology, biology, psychology, linguistics…"

"All interesting class. Problem I give you at start is why you want to jump both shoes into my mind?"

"Huh?"

"If punch face, I punch better. Or put on mask. Can do nothing if you stomp in brain."

"Huh?" Simion is taken aback, like someone just told him to get his hands out of a lady's purse.

"Is hard." Andrei tries to dredge up Paluntov's argument about free will. "What you think is your private. What I think, my private place. Want no stomp. Want no eyes, comment, troll. Private… Friend tell friend, if want, what private thing is in mind. If not want, must be locked door. Yes-no?"

Chastened, Simion rolls it over on his tongue, nodding as the concept coalesces. "Your private thoughts are… private. We all have those things that we must keep that way. So, as you say, when a friend decides to tell you those private things, it is that person's free will to do so."

"Is not free will if someone see everything private. Is dangerous. Get you dead."

Simion is having an epiphany. Stepping over this line, he looks back to see how blind he has been to people around him. Not simply in the matter of wanting to look into their minds. He sees that he was imposing his own will on them in so many ways, without giving it a thought.

"Respect is at the heart of it." He nods again. "Everybody has their own private thoughts and their own desires. If they want – *if they want* – to engage with me as a friend, it is their free will to make that decision."

They sit on their boxes thinking it over.

Andrei flashes an impish grin. "Not all have enough brain for free will."

SEARCHING FOR FATE

From Serbian Folk Songs, Fairy Tales and Proverbs, a collection by Maximillian A Mügge, published by Drane's, London, 1916, with editing by George Opacic

Once upon a time there were two brothers who lived together in a house. The one did all the work, whereas the other one idled about and never did anything but eat and drink. They had an abundance of everything and were blessed with cattle, horses, sheep, pigs and bees.

One day, the brother who did all the work said to himself, "Why should I work so hard for myself and for that lazy-bones as well? It would be much better if we separate. I shall work for myself and he may do what he likes."

And so he told his brother, "It is not fair that I have to manage everything while you never lend me a hand. You think of nothing but eating, drinking and reading. Therefore, I have made up my mind. We need to go our separate ways."

His brother tried to dissuade him, saying, "You have the management of everything, my brother; both your property and mine. And you know I am quite content and agree with everything you do."

But the industrious brother insisted, so the other one had to give in. He said, "Very well. I shall not be cross with you about this. Divide up our shares as you see fit and give me what you think is mine."

Then everything was divided up. The lazy brother took his share and at once appointed a cow-keeper for his cattle, a stable-boy for his horses, a swine-herd, and a bee-keeper, saying to them, "All my property I leave in your hands and God's. You will know best what to do." After that, he stayed at home, unconcerned and without troubling himself about the property that was his, receiving his fair share as owner.

The other brother went on working hard, as before, looking after his own herds alone. He was most careful, yet despite that, he did not thrive but suffered many losses. And his affairs became worse and worse by the day. At last, he was so poor that he did not even have a pair a of shoes to use so he walked about barefoot. Finally he said to himself, "I will go to my brother to see how he is getting on."

His way led him past a meadow in which there was a flock of sheep, and when he drew nearer he saw there was no shepherd, but an exceedingly beautiful maiden who was spinning a golden thread.

He greeted the girl with a friendly, "God be with you." He asked her, "Whose are those sheep?"

She replied, "For whom I belong, his are the sheep."

Then he asker her, "Who are you?"

Whereupon she answered, "I am your brother's Good Luck."

Overcome with great anger, he asked, "Where is *my* Good Luck?"

The maiden replied, "Oh, that is very far from you."

"And could I find it?" he asked.

"You may," she said. "Go and search for it."

When he had heard this, and seeing that his brother's sheep were so fine that he could not possibly imagine sheep more valuable, he was no longer inclined to view the other herds, but went straightaway to his bother's house.

When the latter beheld him he had pity on him and, with tears in his eyes, said, "Where have you been all this time?" Noticing his brother's worn clothes and bare feet, he gave him a pair of good shoes and some money.

After he had been entertained for a few days the poor brother started again for home. Arriving there, he took a knapsack over his shoulders, with as much bread as he had left, took a staff in hand and went off into the Wide World to find his Good Luck.

When he had been walking for some time he came to a dark forest. There he found an ugly old woman sleeping under a shrub. He lifted his stick and poked her in the back to wake her up.

She got up with some difficulty, hardly able to open her blurred eyes. She said, "You may thank God that I had fallen asleep here, for had I been awake you would not have received those lovely shoes."

He asker her, "Who are you that on your account I should not have been given these shoes?"

The old woman said, "I am your Good Luck."

When he heard this he grew very angry, saying, "So *you* are my Good Luck? I wish God would banish you! Who is it that has placed your burden on my shoulders?"

The old hag interrupted him, "Fate has given me onto you."

Then he asked, "Where is this Fate? I would have words with her!"

And she said, "Go forth; search for it!" With those words she disappeared.

Thereupon, the man started again on his way, this time to find Fate.

While he was travelling he came to a village. Near the centre there stood a fine house in which he could see that a large fireplace was burning brightly. He thought to himself, "Here must be a wedding, or they are celebrating a feast-day!"

He entered the house and saw hanging over the fire a big kettle in which the supper was cooking, and the master of the house sat by the fire. He wished the master a good evening, to which the master of the house replied, "May God bestow on you all good things!" Inviting him to take a seat nearby, he asked the traveller who he was and where he was going.

Then the travelling brother told him his story, and how he, too, had been a house-holder, how he had become poor, and that he was now on his way to ask Fate herself why it was that just *he* should remain poor. He asked the master of the house why and for whom he was cooking such a big meal.

The master answered, "Alas! My brother, I am the master of this house and have an abundance of everything, but, nevertheless, I am unable to appease the hunger of my people. It is as though dragons be hidden in their stomachs. Just observe my people when we are at supper; then you will see it."

And when they sat down for supper the men snatched and grabbed one another's food so that in a few minutes the large cauldron was empty. After supper the host's young wife collected all the bones and threw them on a heap behind the stove. As the traveller was wondering at this, suddenly two very old people, thin as skeletons, crawled forth in order to suck the bones.

When the master of the house was asked, "Who are those two behind the stove?"

The master answered, "They are my father and mother and they will not die. It is as though they are chained to this world."

The next morning when they parted, the traveller was requested kindly to ask Fate why the people in his house could not be sufficiently fed, and why his father and mother suffered so long in dying. The traveller promised he would do so, taking his leave to search for Fate.

After he had been on the road for ever so long, one evening he came into another village. He entered one of the houses and asked for a night's shelter. Readily he was received. When he was asked what was his destination he told them his whole story.

Then the people in the house said, "For God's sake, brother, when you have reached your goal, do ask why our cattle do not thrive but are growing thinner and thinner."

He promised to ask Fate about it. The next morning he set out again.

Coming to a fast rushing river he called out, "Oh, Water, Water, carry me over to the other bank."

The water asked him, "Where are you going?"

And he told the water, "I am on a great search for Fate."

Then the water carried him safely across, saying, "Please, brother; ask Fate why there is nothing that can live within me."

The traveller thanked the water and promised to ask Fate.

After ever so long a time, the traveller at last came to a huge green forest. Here he met a blind hermit whom he asked, "My friend, can you offer me any information in my quest to find Fate?"

And the hermit said to him, "Go from here straight across the mountains, then you will arrive exactly in front of Fate's castle. But there, you must not say one word." The hermit wagged a finger. "Not one. Only, at all times, do precisely the same thing Fate is doing, until she puts questions to you."

The traveller thanked the hermit and set out on his journey through the forest and across the mountains.

When he arrived at the castle of Fate, what wonders he did behold! Everywhere was imperial splendour, and a great number of servants, men and women, were hurrying about. But Fate sat quite alone at a table eating her supper.

When the traveller saw her, for whom he had been searching such a long time, he sat down at her side and shared her supper. After supper, Fate laid down to rest. So did he.

Toward midnight there came the most awful noise and turmoil in the castle. Above all the turmoil, a voice clearly sang out. "O Fate! O Fate! One hundred thousand souls have been born today. Give them something according to your pleasure!"

Thereupon, Fate opened a treasure-box full of gold. She took out of it glittering sovereigns and scattered them all over the floor of the great hall. At the same time she said, "As I am faring today, so shall they fare all their lives!"

At daybreak, the magnificent castle was gone. In its place stood a house of modest appearance. Yet there was in it enough, and to spare, of everything. When evening fell, Fate again sat down to supper. So did the traveller, and neither spoke a word. After supper both lay down to rest.

Toward midnight there came again a most awful noise and turmoil. Above all the turmoil, a voice clearly sang out. "O Fate! O Fate! One hundred thousand souls have been born today. Give them something according to your pleasure!"

Then Fate rose, opened a money-box, but inside there were no sovereigns, only silver coins with an occasional gold coin hidden away among them. Fate pulled them out, scattering the silver coins all over the floor of the room. At the same time she said, "As I am faring today, so shall they fare all their lives!"

And at daybreak, that comfortable house was gone too. In its place stood a smaller house. And so it happened each night so that in the morning the house became smaller until at last, there remained nothing but a wretched hut. This time, Fate took a spade and began digging. The traveller also took a spade and they both kept on digging through the day.

When evening fell, Fate took a piece of bread, broke it in half, giving the traveller a half. That was their supper. When they had eaten it they both lay down to rest.

Toward midnight there came again a most awful noise and turmoil. Above all the turmoil, a voice clearly sang out. "O Fate! O Fate! One hundred thousand souls have been born today. Give them something according to your pleasure!"

Then Fate rose, opened a little box, and began scattering small potsherds; among them were a very few coins. At the same time she said, "As I am faring today, so shall they fare all their lives!"

When daybreak next came, the hut had been changed again into a grand palace – just as grand as the one which the traveller had first seen.

And now at last, Fate spoke to him, asking him, "Why did you come here?"

The traveller started to speak, telling Fate the reason for his quest, saying that he wanted to personally ask Fate why she had given him such Bad Luck.

Fate said to him, "You have seen how during the first night I was scattering sovereigns, and you have noticed, I hope, everything that happened during that night. Exactly as I am faring during the night in the course of which a person is born, thus will he or she fare throughout their life. You were born during a night of poverty and therefore you will remain poor as long as you live. Your brother, on the other hand, first saw the light of day on a fortunate night, and he will see fortune until the end of his days. But since you have taken so much trouble to come to me in your quest, I will tell you how you may help yourself. Your brother has a daughter, Milica. She was to be just as fortunate as her father but while she was beside an unfortunate soul, a tragedy occurred to her friend and she is now in a very dark place from which even her good fortune cannot save her. If you return to help her, then fortune may smile on you both. But you must not say that it was you who has acquired the fortune but must always say *it is Milica's!*"

The traveller was still confused so he asked, "Is Fate the same in all lands?"

With a sad frown Fate answered, "A wise question. No, each land has its own Fate. Some live forever in a palace and hand out sovereigns only to families who are their friends. The rest of the people receive potsherds. In some lands, Fate is blind or has withered arms, not knowing and not able to give out her fortune. Our land is blessed with much good fortune."

The traveller thanked Fate and said, "I know of a rich farmer who has more than enough of everything, yet he never succeeds in feeding his household well. At every meal they empty a brewer's copper full of food, and even that is not enough for them. And the father and mother of this farmer, as though they are chained to this earth, have grown quite black with age and shrivelled like ghosts. Yet they cannot die. Therefore he begged me when I was his guest for a night to ask you what is the reason for all that."

Fate replied, "All that happens because he does not honour his father and mother. He just throws food at them behind the stove. If he would put them in a place of honour at his table and hand to them the first glass of wine and the first glass of whisky, they would be content and would soon breathe their last, and the people of the farmer's household would no longer eat so much with such disrespect for what he gives them."

The traveller nodded and asked Fate, "In another village where I stayed a night, a man complained to me that his cattle would not thrive and he asked me to find out from you whose fault that was."

And Fate said, "It is because on the day of the patron saint of his house he slaughters the most wretched cow he has. If, on the other hand, he would, in proper honour of the day, sacrifice one of his very best, his household would be pleased and all the cattle would thrive under their care."

Finally, the traveller also inquired on behalf of the water of the river. "How is it that nothing lives in that water?"

And Fate answered, "It is because the water has not had the oblation of human suffering throughout its course. Were the water to be tamed by the heavy and dangerous work of men, then it would become calmed and full of life. However, be careful not to answer the water until you have been carried safely across or it may drown you!"

Once again he thanked Fate for her kind help, then started on his journey home.

Coming across the mountains and arriving at the hermit's house before dawn, the traveller left him the gift of a lamp he had taken from the castle, which shown only for the hermit's eyes.

He travelled on until he reached the water, where he asked, "Water, would you be so kind, once more, to carry me safely to other side?"

The water rushed by even faster, saying, "Well, what did Fate tell you of my troubles?"

The traveller replied, "First carry me across and then I will tell you." Hardly had the water carried him across than he began running, and when he was a good distance away he yelled, "O Water! It is because you have never been tamed by the work of men and have never seen their sacrifice!"

On hearing this, the water rushed at him over the fields and meadows, and only with great difficulty did he escape. Seeing the flooded fields, all the people living nearby worked very hard to make dams and canals, channeling the great river's water into quiet ponds from which much life grew.

When the traveller came to the village of the man whose cattle were not thriving, the man was already impatiently waiting.

"What news do you bring me, brother? Have you questioned Fate on my behalf?"

Whereupon the traveller replied, "Yes, I have done so. Fate said it was because you always offer up the worst cow on the feast day of your household patron saint, thereby showing your contempt for tradition. If you would join your heart in the celebration with your family, all your cattle would thrive."

On hearing this, the farmer said, "Brother, stay with us please. It is but three days to the feast of our patron saint, and if that is true which you tell me, I will show you my gratitude."

When the feast day came, the father of the family prepared his finest bullock and from that moment onwards, his cattle and his household thrived. The following day, the man gave the traveller five oxen as a present and the traveller set out again.

His path home took him into the village where the ever hungry household was. The master of the house greeted him, "For God's sake, tell me, brother; how are you and what did Fate say to you?"

The traveller said, "Fate says the answer to your troubles is that you have not been honouring your father and mother, and you always throw the food at them behind the stove. If you would put them at the table, and moreover, seat them at the place of honour at the top of the table, hand them the first glass of wine and the first glass of whisky, the others of your household would not treat your food and other offerings with such disrespect, and your father and mother would leave this earth in contentment."

When the master of the house heard this he told his wife that his father and mother should be washed and combed and made comfortable. At the evening supper, the father and mother were placed at the top of the table and each was offered the first glass of wine and the first glass of whisky. From that moment onwards, the rest of the household treated each other with respect and did not eat or drink to excess. The father and mother laid down quietly in a few days and died peacefully. Then the grateful master gave the traveller two bullocks, with which the traveller, thanking his host, carried on down the path to his home.

When the traveller finally arrived back at the valley of his home, his neighbours met him, asking, "Whose are these beautiful cattle?"

He said, "My friends, these belong to my brother's daughter, Milica."

When he arrived home he went at once to his brother, greeting him and saying, "My brother, I know that your daughter will not speak nor eat. I beg you to let me help Milica. I wish to have her live with me so that I can save her soul from the darkness that has enveloped her."

"Brother, even the Good Luck that I have been born with has begun to whither away. The maiden no longer spins her golden thread but sits wistfully staring at the clouds. If you say you are able to help my lovely daughter, she is yours. Take Milica with you."

The brother then led Milica to his house. Seated by the fireplace, he told Milica the story of his very long journey and all the people that he had met and how he had been told by Fate how to help them all. And Milica opened her eyes and saw that she was no longer alone and she loved her uncle as her father. From that moment onwards they both prospered much, joining once again the two households of the brothers, with each helping the other.

With everything he gained, the one brother said, "It is Milica's!"

One day, years later, he went out to his fields to see how the corn was growing. It was most lovely to look at the golden silk of all the corn. When a wanderer came along, asking him, "Whose is this lovely corn field?"

The brother, forgetting himself for a moment, said, "It is mine."

In the moment he spoke, flames burst out of the corn and the fire spread rapidly. Quickly he ran after the fleeing wanderer and exclaimed, "Stop, my friend! The corn does not belong to me at all. It is Milica's!"

At once the fire ceased.

Henceforth, he lived happily with Milica running his household and his fields prospered as did his brother's to the end of their days.

THE CUB

In the cold, glaring, low-level Arctic sun, Andrei and Simion grunt crisply, the bitter cold crystalizing each sound as if their grunts have become icy word-forms, ready to fall and fracture on the ground. A minimum of frosty-covered noses peek out of encrusted hoods as they each lean into an unpredictable, turbulent wind. They are barely able to control a tall wobbling mast from two sides, holding scavenged guy-wires. A third guy-wire from the mast has already been secured into the rocks. Their bright orange coveralls are dirty, marked with random streaks of oils and paint from barrels they have been pushing against. Andrei keeps glancing at Simion; he shakes his head at the grimaces on Simion's face with each use of his left arm. He is somehow angry at Simion for getting hurt, and angry that he is angry.

From two sides of the mast, they are pulling hard to draw a ten-metre-long antenna mast up to vertical. Simion's left arm is tightly wrapped in a sling, so he is forced to pull with one-and-a-half hands.

The heavy wind sends hard bits of crystal snow or sand twanging off metal parts as the random gusts bend and whip the steel pole. The mast holds a patched-together antenna, making for an unstable top-heavy load. The bottom end of the pole grinds into a rocky hole. The thicker com cable is loose, attached only to the antenna, and the wind slams it around the pole and guy-wires. During one of its traverses it waves grandly in the wind, describing a wide arc that comes back to smack Simion on the cheek.

"Get the…! " He angrily waves his head at the cable, still pulling on the guy-wire with his good gloved hand, while grabbing the loose end under his boot. "If it ain't one friggen thing up here it's another!" He rubs his cheek awkwardly with his shoulder where a welt is forming. The wayward cable continues its grand arcs, twanging off the third guy-wire.

Continuing to struggle, Simion yells at another gust, "Gimme a break, damnit!" And the wind, at his command, takes a longer break between blasts.

Grinning, Andrei yells, "You want I should shoot it, Simion?"

Pushed to the limit, still hauling the guy-wire, Simion loudly recites into the now lowering wind, "I cordially invite you to go forth and AUTO-PROLIFERATE! Profusely!"

"What you mean, auto prof… What this mean?"

"Ain't telling."

Andrei stops, letting his guy-wire slip back through his gloves. On his side, Simion nearly gets pulled off the ground with one arm, as another strong blast catches the antenna.

"Oww! Andrei! Stop farting around! We need this thing up for reception!" Simion grimaces with pain from his left arm.

Gritting his teeth with exertion and sudden regret, Andrei strengthens his grip on his guy-wire again, steadying the swaying pole. The antenna wobbles ominously, and with each slow shudder the malevolent cable slaps Simion on the head. And then again.

"Ah for chrissake!" He ducks his head down into the collar of his fur coat, blindly pulling the guy-wire. It tautens. He pokes his head out of the hood, looking for the loose cable. Andrei has it in one hand, his other hand is securely holding his own guy-wire.

Simion yells out, "Thanks Andrei. Ok, hold on while I tie this end down."

A turnbuckle has already been attached to where they had calculated the length of the cable should be able to hook into a metal stake driven into the rocks and icy sand. Simion slips his hand down toward the turnbuckle.

"Good. The dangle of the hypotenuse equals 5." He awkwardly puts the turnbuckle's hook through a hole in the stake.

"What you profusely say?!" Andrei is getting exasperated with Simion's unorthodox use of English. He jerks his end of the guy-wire, shaking the antenna.

Still wary of a surprise gust, Simion yells to him, "Andrei, I was just talking about the 3-4-5 triangle we used to calculate the length of this thing. Ok? Remember the square of the hypotenuse?"

Enlightened, Andrei nods.

Simion wipes his nose on the bandage poking out the end of his left sleeve. "After your side is hooked in, we can tighten the turnbuckles to keep the mast vertical. Sort of." He adds, nodding pointedly at the pole bending in the gusts, "And yes, I still think we need a fourth wire to hold against this Arctic hurricane."

Andrei agrees, "Must find more."

Between gusts, a distant but familiar yelp picks up both their heads.

"Stay there Andrei! Where's the rifle?" Simion looks around the rolling tundra.

"Is there." Andrei nods sharply toward a box with their tools on it. As he does so, his hand slides down the wire and he quickly attaches the turnbuckle to his stake.

Running, Simion points a gloved hand away from the flat area of the disused DEW-line base. On the tundra, about a hundred metres away, the young bear cub is coming, working into the wind. It is ranging with its head back and forth, tongue hanging out to one side, moving its little legs robotically, but stumbling every once in a while. The ragged cub closes the distance toward Simion and Andrei.

A glint off to the left of the cub catches his eye, causing Simion to slip on the frosty rocks. Getting back on focus, he rises to his feet and reaches the toolbox. He flicks off the safety and shoulders the rifle stock awkwardly, aiming at the cub. Ignoring the pain of his left arm, Simion holds the weight up as steadily as he can while squinting along the sights. With the movable sight already adjusted down, he waits for the target to get into range.

As the little cub struggles closer, Simion drops the barrel a bit. He sees that it is very thin and dirty. Sniffing high with every few head sways, the cub plods right for a mound of fur and flesh that used to be his mother. The mound has been ravaged by foxes or wild dogs. Blindly yelping as he nuzzles against the fur that is left, he stumbles again, going down over folded front legs, his now bloodied head sinks onto the frozen sand next to his mother.

The rifle lowers off Simion's shoulder. Silent tears swell in his eyes.

Andrei walks up, takes the rifle from Simion, aims and BANG! shoots the cub. It hardly shudders. Shocked, Simion slams against Andrei, knocking him down onto his back on the frosted sand. The rifle stays in Andrei's hands, dry and clean, above his chest.

Crying, "What the hell did you have to do that for? Goddamnit! It's just a little cub!"

From the ground, Andrei shakes his head slowly. "Was dying. We kill his mother."

He carefully gets back up and puts the rifle down on the box, barrel and trigger pointed away from the wind. Simion hovers in the same spot, breathing hard, staring at the sand where Andrei had been, a tear hardening on his frozen red cheek.

MOEBIUS SLIP

A morality play

EXT. W. HASTINGS/ W. PENDER ST., VANCOUVER – LATE AFTERNOON

A huge wall of brown and green ivy, just starting to bud back to life in the spring, is over thirty feet high.

A young woman's torso flashes by the wall. She is half-running on a concrete pedestrian overpass eighty feet west of the ivy wall.

She tosses her short blonde hair out of her serious eyes. The shoulders of her red, yellow and black track suit swish steadily back and forth.

Her black pants get to the stairs going south, then her short legs machine down the steps in one long glide.

At the bottom, her well-used, formerly white running shoes leap the last two steps to land running on the granite pavement.

She slows to a fast walk as she gets to the sidewalk beside West Pender St. She heads west.

Angled sunlight slashes at her face from between tall glass buildings.

GAEAL KRAFT is twenty, a centimetre-shorter-than-a-metre-an-a-quarter and ready to take on the world. Her confident, quick stride eats up space.

Ahead of Gaeal down the sidewalk she notices an older, portly man struggling under the weight of a heavy cloth bag in his left hand and a heavier black leather briefcase slung over his right shoulder.

As she gains ground on him, he totters towards a long step next to a building and collapses sideways against his briefcase which drops onto the long step.

Gaeal slows down.

From the edge of the sidewalk,

GAEAL

> Are you all right?
>
> (reaches for her clipped-on
> cellphone)
> Do you want me to
> call for help?

SAM ELDRIDGE is wheezing hard. He turns toward Gaeal slowly, sweat beading on his high forehead and forming a stain under his

arms. His cream-colored shirt is rolled up
at the sleeves. A tie is pulled wide at his
throat. Suspenders hold up his ample grey
striped pants.

SAM

WHEEZE WHEEZE

Sam's high pitched English accent takes
Gaeal by surprise.

SAM

> Would you mind so
> much...*WHEEZE* helping
> me to carry... *WHEEZE*
> this bag down the
> block? *WHEEZE*
>
> It's these books
> that've done me in...
> *WHEEZE*

He limply holds the handles of the cloth
bag, which is slipping off the shoulder
strap of the briefcase. The cloth handles
are soaked with his sweat. She jumps back.

GAEAL

> Get out of my face
> you dirty old man! Of
> all the...

She steps back further, but slips with one foot on the edge of the sidewalk as a passing blue pickup truck with the name DOLCE LANDSCAPING on the door honks at her and the side mirror smashes into her shoulder, sending Gaeal careening down the sidewalk to lay in a pile next to the building.

Sam has raised his hand to warn her, too late, and he still holds it up, labouriously pivoting toward her as she crashes to the pavement.

The driver looks through his rear window past the pile of yard waste in his truck, with fear on his face. He takes off.

SAM

Oh my god!

Sam pushes hard to get up, leaving the bag and briefcase where they lay. He wheezes over to Gaeal, dropping awkwardly onto one knee next to her.

Gaeal has cuts on her head that are bleeding heavily. Her eyes are closed. Sam sees from her chest that she is breathing in short, choppy breaths.

Sam looks around, but the truck has disappeared and no one else is close.

He sees her cellphone clipped to her pants waist. Fumbling with the clip, he pulls it off.

>>>> SAM

> How do these things work?…

He presses a 9 and sees "911" on the screen. Not knowing what else to do, he looks at the phone in frustration for a few seconds, then he hears it dialling by itself.

He hears the 911 OPERATOR,

>>>> **911 OPERATOR V.O.**

> Emergency services, do you need an ambulance, fire or police?

Sam puts the phone up to his ear awkwardly.

>>>> SAM

> Hello? Hello, is this the emergency operator?

911 OPERATOR V.O.

Yes sir. Do you need an ambulance, fire or police?

SAM

I'm on, oh, I think it's Pender, West Pender and a young lady's been hit by a car, by a, what do call them, pickup truck!

She needs an ambulance and the police should be after that idiot who didn't stop!…

911 OPERATOR V.O.

Yes sir. I'll transfer you to the ambulance dispatch right away. Please stay on the line.

Telephone sounds: CLICK, STATIC, CLICKS

The AMULANCE DISPATCH comes on.

AMBULANCE DISPATCH V.O.

Ambulance services,
what is the nature of
your emergency?

Sam rolls his eyes, speaking louder and
more slowly,

SAM

I SAID, A YOUNG LADY
HAS BEEN HIT BY A
PICKUP TRUCK AND SHE
IS BLEEDING ALL OVER
THE PAVEMENT. WILL
YOU PLEASE JUST SEND
AN AMBULANCE!?

AMBULANCE DISPATCH V.O.

Yes sir. Where is she
now?

SAM

ON THE PAVEMENT! You
bloody fool!

AMBULANCE DISPATCH V.O.

Sir, what address? Is
she outside of a
building?

SAM

Oh! I'm sorry, yes.
We're on West Pender…

He raises his head to look back up the
street.

SAM

About a block, ah,
west of Burrard.

AMBULANCE DISPATCH V.O.

That's in downtown
Vancouver?

SAM

WELL OF *COURSE* IT'S
IN BLOODY DOWNTOWN
VANCOUVER…

Sorry. I'm sorry,
yes. Downtown
Vancouver, just west
of Burrard. Hurry
please!

AMBULANCE DISPATCH V.O.

Sir, an ambulance has
been dispatched. Can
you stay with the
victim?

> ### SAM
>
> Huh? Oh! Of course!
> I'll be right here.

> ### AMBULANCE DISPATCH V.O.
>
> Sir, do you mind
> giving me your name
> and your cellphone
> number?

> ### SAM
>
> This isn't my
> telephone. It's hers.
> My name is Sam
> Eldridge…

> ### AMBULANCE DISPATCH V.O.
>
> Thank you, sir. The
> ambulance should be
> there in a few
> minutes.

SOUND: SIREN approaching.

<u>EXT. STREET — SEVERAL MINUTES LATER</u>

The paramedics are closing the door of
their ambulance, one inside and one out.
The outside paramedic moves quickly to get
in the front door. The ambulance takes off,
siren sounding.

Behind Sam, an unkempt young man with a bulging garbage bag picks up Sam's briefcase and walks away with it.

Sam is standing on the sidewalk absently holding onto Gaeal's cellphone. He looks at it in his hand, quickly raises his other hand toward the ambulance.

                    SAM
          WAIT!

But they are long gone.

Not knowing what to do with it, he stuffs the cellphone into a pocket. Then he looks around quickly.

                    SAM
          My bags!

Sam sees his cloth book-bag, but the black leather briefcase is missing.

Walking much faster than he ever has, Sam gets to his book-bag and puts the spilled-out ledger books back into it.

He sees his briefcase on the thief's shoulder half a block away. The thief is walking nonchalantly. Sam is about to yell, but stops, gets up and starts off down the sidewalk, wheezing more and more as he gets closer to the thief. The thief crosses against a light.

Sam recklessly crosses at the intersection, avoiding a car whose driver honks at him and points aggressively up at the signal light.

Sam reaches the other side and bends over, wheezing hard. Getting some breath back, he takes up the pursuit again.

At the next intersection, the thief is stopped for traffic. Almost reaching the THIEF, Sam snatches for his back, hits the full, light garbage bag, then lunges past it. The thief hears Sam's wheezing and spins away.

> **THIEF**
> Bugger off old man!
> That's MY stuff!

He protects his garbage bag, spinning around and jumping back from Sam. The traffic clears.

> **SAM**
> You… *WHEEZE* … stole
> my… *WHEEZE* …
> briefcase!

                          THIEF

            Go fucken pound salt,

            Fatass! *I* found it!

            YOU want one, go

            fucken find your own!

        (grins, looking Sam up-and-down)

            OLD man! You're fat

            enough to feed me for

            a year!

The thief looks around, and, seeing nobody
nearby, pulls out a knife. He slowly slices
the air.

                          THIEF

            Got any money on you,

            old man?

Sam remembers the cellphone in his pocket.
He pulls it out and punches the 9 while
backing away from the thief.

The thief lunges forward, cutting Sam
across the arm holding the cellphone. The
phone drops as Sam yells,

                           SAM

            AHHHHH! HELP!

            Somebody help!

The thief reaches for the phone but a siren
comes on as a police car screams around the

corner. The thief drops his knife,
awkwardly running with his load down an
alley.

A door on the police car flies open. A
female police officer runs after the thief,
who turns around, jumps as he sees the cop,
drops his garbage bag and the briefcase and
runs hard up the alley. The cop stops at
the bags, puffing.

The other cop, JAMAL, looks around from his
door then runs over to Sam.

The female cop, SUE, opens the garbage bag
tentatively, glancing at the bottles and
cans that spill out.

Leaving them, she picks up the briefcase
and walks quickly back to Sam.

Jamal slips on plastic gloves to attend to
Sam.

JAMAL

> Sir, are you badly
> cut?...

Sam looks dumbly at his bleeding arm,
holding it half out so the blood doesn't
get on his clothes. Jamal yells back over
his shoulder.

JAMAL

SUE! GET A WIDE
DRESSING AND TAPE
FROM THE TRUNK!

(back to Sam)
Sir, we'll put a
dressing on that and
call for an
ambulance.

(he speaks into his shoulder mike)
227, we need an
ambulance for a knife
wound, corner of West
Pender and Homer... HOW
long?...

INT. HOSPITAL LOBBY – LATER THAT EVENING

Sam is giving his book-bag and briefcase to
a young man who nervously looks around at
the police. Sam's arm is bandaged. The
young man leaves quickly.

Sam watches the young man exit, until he
gets right into a waiting car that takes
off immediately.

Turning, Sam goes to the information desk.

The information CLERK finishes with a
previous customer.

CLERK

May I help you?

Sam holds up his bandaged arm.

SAM

Yes, please. As you
see I was involved in
an accident earlier
and I need to return
this telephone to a
young lady who was
also involved.

She was short, about
twenty…

CLERK

I'm sorry sir, I have
no idea who was
admitted. Have you
checked at Emergency?
She may still be
there.

SAM

Of course. Thank you
very much.

Emergency is…?

The clerk looks at Sam quizzically.

> **CLERK**
>
> Straight down those stairs, turn right at the bottom.

INT. EMERGENCY — MINUTES LATER

In the busy waiting area, Sam is speaking to one of the triage nurses. She shrugs and waves him away, calling the next patient up.

Sam wanders past waiting people, over to the pay telephones on the wall.

He digs out coins from his pocket, still awkwardly holding the cellphone. He finally shoves it into a pocket as he holds the payphone handset.

Sam keys in a number that he reads off a card.

> **SAM**
>
> Hello? Yes, I was wondering if you could give me some information about a young lady who was just admitted to the Emergency department…

Looking at the reception desk, Sam sees the person who has picked up a phone. He sees her speak as he hears her answer on the telephone.

SAM

> I was brought in from
> the same incident,
> but it was the police
> who drove me in…
>
> Yes, she came in an
> ambulance. I have the
> young lady's mobile
> telephone and I
> wanted to return it…
>
> Well, if you look
> over at the telephone
> booths in your lobby,
> I'll wave at you…
>
> That's right.

Smiling, he waves at the triage nurse then hangs up the phone.

Walking with some trouble, he gets over to the desk, then leans heavily on the counter.

Sam places the cellphone in front of the surprised nurse.

<u>INT. HOSPITAL WARD - THAT EVENING</u>

Sam is sitting in a chair at the bedside of Gaeal. She has her head bandaged and is still groggy.

Sam puts her cellphone on the table beside her bed.

                    SAM

          We've had a rather
          exciting night, my
          dear. And I don't
          even know your name…

Gaeal moves her head gingerly.

                    GAEAL

          Who the heck are you?

          Ohh. My shoulder…

She grimaces. Sam puts his bandaged arm up so she can see it. She notices the bandages and gives Sam a questioning raised eyebrow.

Sam smiles at her.

                    SAM

          My name is Sam
          Eldridge. We were on
          West Pender when a
          car, a pickup truck

        hit you. I used your
        telephone...

(he nods at the cellphone on the desk)
        to call for an
        ambulance. Then a
        creature of the
        streets stole my
        briefcase. In running
        him down - well, yes,
        that was rather a
        slow motion chase...

(he pats his prominent belly)
        when I caught up to
        him, he expressed
        some displeasure at
        being relieved of my
        briefcase and he
        slashed me with a
        knife. I am afraid I
        had to resort to
        using your telephone
        again to summon the
        constabulary. I will,
        of course, recompense
        you the cost of using
        your telephone.

Gaeal can't help smiling, despite her headache. The grin elicits a grimace. She puts her hand up to ask for a minute's pause.

Composing herself, Gaeal speaks quietly.

                    GAEAL
          Thanks for returning
          my phone. Did you say
          Sam?

       (he nods as she adjusts herself on the
        bed)
          Have to find out what
          happened to me. Is
          there a nurse?...

She slowly moves her head around, seeing only the other beds in the ward.

Sam leans forward.

                    SAM
          I will call a nurse
          for you, but as I
          said, you were struck
          by a vehicle which
          sent you to onto the
          pavement...

She holds her hand up again.

GAEAL

> Yes, so you say.
> Please find a nurse
> for me.

> (she looks at his bandaged arm)
> What happened to you?
> Did I fight back?

Sam is confused.

SAM

> I beg your pardon?
> Ah, as I said a thief
> slashed my arm.

Gaeal sees a NURSE enter the ward and waves to her.

The nurse surveys patients quickly as she makes her way to Gaeal's bed.

NURSE

> And how are you
> feeling now, ah...

> (she looks at her chart)
> Gaeal? Oh, I see Mr.
> Eldridge has returned
> your cellphone. Mr.
> Eldridge, would you
> mind taking a seat
> over by the desk? I

need to ask Gaeal a
few questions.

Sam takes a moment to recognize that he is
being shooed away.

SAM

Oh! Yes. Very sorry,
nurse. Ah, if I may,
ah, Gaeal, I would
appreciate it if you
would contact me
later. Here is my
card.

(he places his business card beside
 the cellphone)
I do feel responsible
for your predicament
and would very much
wish to repay you in
some way.

(he gets up painfully, using his good
 arm)
When you feel better.

INT. SAM'S OFFICE, SEVERAL DAYS LATER

Sam is having an animated conversation with a rich-suited, middle-aged man. The young fellow who had taken away Sam's bags at the hospital is standing patiently by the office door. The middle-aged man, GELLERT, is a formidable-looking former soccer player. He speaks with a slight Hungarian accent. Sam is sweating, but determined to hold his own in the discussion.

SAM

As you may plainly see, Gellert, I am in poor health and this knife wound has become infected.

(he shows Gellert a bottle of pills on his desk)

I am simply no longer in a position to continue with our contract.

(Gellert tries to interrupt)

No, I must insist, my friend. You may threaten me bodily

> harm, if you wish,
> but in all honesty,
> whether it be a
> friend of yours...

(he looks over at the other man)

> or my own body, I
> fear I am not long
> for this mortal soil.
> I ask you kindly to
> put me out to pasture
> so that I may spend a
> few peaceful days
> under the sun.

(his chair creaks loudly as he leans
 back)

> I would have
> absolutely no reason
> to tattle to the
> authorities regarding
> your, ah, extensive
> business enterprises.
> Non whatsoever. I
> place myself at your
> mercy, knowing that,
> at heart, you have a
> kind soul and have
> appreciated the work
> that I have done on

> your behalf. As you
> well know, my
> endeavours have
> resulted in a
> significant benefit
> to you. Allow me this
> one small favour in
> return.

The young man at the door rolls his eyes,
then is surprised to hear his boss' answer.

Gellert tents his fingers impatiently, then
makes a decision.

GELLERT
> Sam, you know I
> appreciate what you
> have done for me...
> Ok. Listen. You may
> retire. Are you
> confident that,
> whats-his-name, Chan,
> will be a good and
> willing accountant
> for me?

SAM
> Absolutely. He will
> be better than I
> could be, since he

has been tutored
extensively at two of
the highest ranked...

GELLERT

Fine. I trust your
choice. You know that
I have always left
the books up to you.

Ok. I have that place
in St. Lucia. It is
yours. The only thing
I want of you there
is that you help with
the occasional
deposit. Our bank,
there - well, you
know the routine... I
think you will need
to be made a
director. Please see
to that. When do you
want to go?

EXT. SEAWALL, NEXT WEEK, MORNING

Sam waddles for a short stretch of the Seawall east of Cambie Street Bridge. He is dressed somewhat incongruously in new duds: bright white tee-shirt trimmed in lime-green, with large, flappy, beige shorts, and neon-orange runners. His white legs barely look strong enough to hold the bulk under his triple-extra large clothes.

Having gone all the way down the ramp to the Seawall and at least fifty metres of the Seawall, Sam is sweating profusely.

> **SAM**
>> That's it. Too much
>> of a good thing can
>> be dangerous. *Wheeze.*
>> Time for a rest.

He heads for a bench and plops down, wiping his forehead.

Sam is content to sit and watch the oh-so energetic young people trot by. After a while he recognizes a familiar face and calls out.

> **SAM**
>> Gaeal!

Stopping in her tracks, Gaeal thinks it is one of her friends but is disappointed when she sees the fat old man had called out. Reluctantly, Gaeal steps over to the bench.

                    GAEAL

          Hey there...

                    SAM

          Sam.

                    GAEAL

          Right! Sam. How are
          you doing. Did that
          knife wound heal up?

Smiling and indicating the seat next to him on the bench,

                    SAM

               Yes, thank you for
               asking, Gaeal. More
               importantly, how are
               YOU doing? That must
               have been a nasty
               gash to your head.

She tentatively takes a seat on the far edge of the bench.

                    GAEAL

               Oh, it's healing. I
               just have to keep my

             hair down over my
             forehead.

She smiles as she lifts her hair up to show
her wound line.

                    GAEAL

             Only four stitches. I
             wished they'd used
             glue or something.
             The doctor says it'll
             basically go away
             after a while.

Sam politely replies,

                    SAM

             I don't even notice
             it. Oh! Didn't you
             have blond hair at
             the time?

She fluffs her hair to have it fall back
over her forehead.

                    GAEAL

             Yeah. My hairdresser
             suggested this darker
             shade would be better
             to cover the, ah,
             cut.

Sam shifts his weight to better talk to her.

> **SAM**
>
> Well, that certainly is an attractive colour, my dear. She did your lovely features justice.

She bats her eyes.

> **GAEAL**
>
> He.

> **SAM**
>
> I'm sorry?

> **GAEAL**
>
> My hairdresser is Jonathan. He has a very chic salon...

> **SAM**
>
> Oh! On Robson? I know it well.

Gaeal is very surprised.

> **SAM**
>
> A business acquaintance. Of an acquaintance. But I

> digress. I am leaving
> that business life
> behind. I was
> persuaded to hang up
> my spreadsheet.
> Before you, my dear,
> is a retired
> accountant. My
> lifelong investments
> will allow me to
> retire in
> considerable comfort
> in the Caribbean.

He leans back and takes a deep breath, contented. Then he remembers a task that is yet to be accomplished.

SAM

> Oh! My dear! Perhaps
> you would care to
> join me for lunch? I
> do wish to offer you
> some small payback
> for what I so
> foolishly put you
> through. If you
> agree, the Hotel
> Chelsea has a

                    pleasant little
                    restaurant.

Gaeal turns to the fat old man, ready to
brush him off, then stops to think.

                    GAEAL
                    I'm not looking for
                    money, ah, Mr.
                    Embridge?

                    SAM
                    Eldridge, my dear.
                    But please just call
                    me Sam. Sam I am, as
                    someone once said.

                    GAEAL
                    Mr. Eldridge. Sam.
                    Yes, thank you. I
                    would be delighted to
                    have lunch with you.
                    Hotel Chelsea? Isn't
                    that a bit expensive?

Slapping his knees happily,

                    SAM
                    Not at all, my dear.
                    Not at all. I have
                    acquaintances there,
                    as well. In fact, I

> will take this
> opportunity to advise
> them that they will
> be dealing with my
> successor. Excellent!

INT. HOTEL CHELSEA RESTAURANT, THAT NOON

Sam has changed into what he believes is business casual. He exits the elevator into an opulent restaurant at the top of the boutique hotel. The maître d', VINCENT, almost does not recognize him.

VINCENT

> Sir! You should not
> do this to an old
> man. My heart is
> skipping. I know that
> you have never before
> been in public
> without a tie and
> suit!

Sam grins and keeps walking to HIS booth with a magnificent view of Burrard Inlet. Vincent follows closely, being sure to pull the table out for Sam, then politely adjusts it.

Seated comfortably, Sam grins slyly at
Vincent.

                    SAM

          Vincent, I will not
          likely be returning
          to your fine and
          over-priced
          establishment.

Vincent is upset.

                    VINCENT

          Sir! If I have
          slighted you in the
          least; if one my
          staff has so much
          as...

                    SAM

          No, no. Please calm
          down, Vincent. No
          need to get the brass
          knuckles out on
          anyone here. Your
          service has always
          been most
          satisfactory.

               (he looks down at his belly and pats
               it)

If anything, overly
satisfactory. No,
Vincent, I am
retiring!

Vincent looks at him like Sam has just
committed hari kari.

VINCENT

Ah, sir...

(he glances around nervously)
Does...

SAM

Gellert know? Yes,
Vincent. Our
Protector not only
knows, he has given
me the villa on St.
Lucia for my
retirement.

(remembering)
Oh! A young lady will
be joining me
shortly. Please treat
her kindly. She is
recovering from a...
well, a wound.

Vincent does his best to suppress a leer.

VINCENT

Yes, sir. I
understand.

SAM

No, you do not!

I owe her a good meal
and I may offer her
some money for my
having caused her
injury.

(quietly)
I may need a few
hundred in fifties,
if you...

Vincent puts a finger to his lips.

VINCENT

Say what you need and
it shall be in your
hands.

Sam notices Gaeal exit the elevator. He
nods to Vincent.

SAM

She has arrived.

Vincent pirouettes gracefully to greet
Gaeal.

With a slight bow,

VINCENT

Welcome to our humble
eatery. My name is
Vincent. If you would
care to follow me?...

Gaeal is in awe of the splendid
accoutrements. She nods absently, following
Vincent while staring around, then out the
windows at the view.

At Sam's table, she is embarrassed.

GAEAL

Mr. Eldridge...

SAM

Please. Sam.

He indicates the seat which Vincent has
pulled out for her.

GAEAL

Sam. I feel so under-
dressed. I just threw
on a sweater...

SAM

My dear, please. Have
a seat. And may I say

> that your sweater is
> lovely.

> (looking up at Vincent)
> Isn't it, Vincent?

Vincent is admiring the contents of the
sweater.

VINCENT

> Oh, most assuredly,
> sir. Her sweater
> is... lovely.

Defensively, Gaeal pulls her sweater
closed.

GAEAL

> Nice view up here.

She sits down and adjusts herself primly in
the seat.

Sam smiles deprecatingly.

SAM

> You must excuse
> Vincent, my dear. We
> do not let him out
> very often.

Vincent grins.

VINCENT

May I bring you a
glass of wine to
start your meal?

Gaeal and Sam speak at the same time.

SAM

Yes, please.

GAEAL

Oh, no thank... ah...
Well, if Sam is
having...

VINCENT

Perhaps a delightful
Rosé, to match your
sweater?

GAEAL

Oh! Yes, please. If
that's alright with
Sam?

Vincent smiles.

VINCENT

My pleasure. We have
a perfect Rosé,
chilled.

(to Sam)

>   It is from, ah, our
>   friend's new
>   acquisition in the
>   Okanagan. I am sure
>   you will find it a
>   pleasant vintage.

The meal proceeds, with Sam not having to
order while Gaeal chooses carefully at
first, then, encouraged by both Sam and
Vincent, with joy.

Finishing the meal, Sam pats his tummy.

SAM

>   I must apologize, my
>   dear. I had fully
>   intended to start a
>   very strict diet. And
>   yet, in these
>   pleasant
>   surroundings, in the
>   company of a young
>   lady who so much
>   enjoys her life and
>   truly glows because
>   of it...

Gaeal gives him a stern look but cannot
maintain it for more than a few seconds.
She bursts out into a laugh.

                    GAEAL

          I hope you're not
          flirting with me,
          Sam.

He returns a kindly smile.

                    SAM

          Alas, my dear, if I
          were to shed fifty
          years and two hundred
          pounds, it would be
          my distinct pleasure
          to flirt with you.

     (shaking his head sadly)
          No. I fully realize
          my many limitations.
          I shall content
          myself with offering
          you the gratification
          of a fine meal and,
          if I may be so crass
          as to broach the
          subject, a small
          payment...

She is about to protest but he holds up a
hand.

SAM

> A small payment to
> cover the loss you
> must have incurred
> over the past few
> weeks.

Gaeal wants to reject the offer, then thinks about it.

GAEAL

> You are a very kind
> man, Sam. I thank you
> for the offer. This
> meal has been
> fantastic... You
> know, I, well, I am
> behind in my rent
> because of being off
> work. They've been
> prissy in the past...

SAM

> My dear, I am
> devastated. I must
> insist on covering
> this month's rent for
> you. How much is
> that?

Gaeal is tempted.

GAEAL

My god. I certainly
could use it.

Just to get back on
my feet. But even
half would be a great
help.

Could you afford, say
eight hundred?

Sam sits back.

SAM

My dear. Gaeal. I do
not want you to feel
there is any
obligation
whatsoever. I am
pleased to give you
one thousand dollars

(she stiffens)

purely as recompense
to my thoughtless
actions on that day.
I was devastated when
I caused you to back
into that vehicle. As
you lay bleeding on

> the pavement, I could
> only wish it had been
> me, instead.

He clicks his fingers to Vincent, who has
been within earshot and comes from his desk
with an envelope.

Sam receives the envelope then passes it to
Gaeal, patting her hand as he does so.

SAM

> I ask you not to open
> it at this time,
> please, Gaeal. Merely
> accept it with my
> sincere apologies.

GAEAL

> Ah... Ok... Well,
> thank you so much,
> Sam. I really do
> appreciate it. This
> will certainly help.

They finish the meal. Gaeal is accompanied
by Sam to the elevator. She has the
envelope in one hand as she gives Sam an
impulsive peck on the cheek.

After the door closes Sam turns to Vincent.

                    SAM

          How much did you put
          in the envelope,
          Vincent?

Vincent keeps his face serious.

                  VINCENT

          She was a damsel in
          distress. So I put in
          some hundreds.

                    SAM

          How many, Vincent?

                  VINCENT

          Twenty. Or so. I only
          had time to scoop a
          bunch out of the
          drawer.

Shaking his head with a smile.

                    SAM

          Vincent. I hope she
          doesn't get the wrong
          idea... Anyway, I
          will tell Chan how to
          make the adjustments.

                  VINCENT

          Chan?

SAM

> Oh, yes. Allow me to
> fill you in...

EXT. SEAWALL, NEXT DAY, MORNING

Sam has given up on running the Seawall again. He is seated on the same bench, dressed in new, but equally incongruous exercise clothes.

As he watches the parade of runners, one of them comes directly up to him. The RUNNER is visibly angry. She opens a small backpack and roughly spills its contents onto Sam's lap.

RUNNER

> She told me this is
> where she met you,
> you fucken son of a
> bitch!

The runner stands over Sam as he sputters out a reply.

SAM

What? What are you
doing? What is all
this? Who are you?

The runner fairly spits out her answer.

RUNNER

This is what Gaeal
bought with your
blood money! It's the
last thing she ever
touched. It's a
needle and drug shit,
you son of a bitch!

I know who you are.
You're the fat slob
who cooks the books
for the mob! Well,
here is what that
blood money does to
us poor people on the
street! FOR REAL!
Your gang just killed
another poor, lovely
young girl! She's now
just another number;
one of four, today!
And every bloody day!

Go fucken enjoy your
blood money and uber-
genteel lifestyle in
some villa on a sandy
white beach! YOUR
KIND MAKE ME SICK
ENOUGH TO THROW UP
ALL OVER YOU!

BOXES

Tong Gia Doi is at a bank in the line.

He sees an attractive sign for loans and makes a snap decision to see the loans manager.

Tong agrees to a quick arrangement for $30,000. At the counter, a counting machine spews the cash in a blinding stream directly into his open backpack.

On his route home he stops at a steel plate supplier. The retail counter very helpfully fills his order. He uses part of the cash to buy 6 pieces of precut steel that come in a package. He takes the rest of the cash and the steel home in his backpack.

Eagerly, Tong goes into his garage with the steel plates. He carefully cleans the pieces of heavy gauge steel then, satisfied, welds the sides and bottom into a beautiful rectangular box. Standing back to admire the fine symmetry of his box, he is getting excited. The next stage is trimming out the interior with long-lasting pseudocloth and Barcelonan leather. The interior sparkles and looks fantastic when he is done.

Tong puts the remaining cash, about $29,900, carefully inside the trimmed-out box. With due ceremony, he then welds the top shut with the last piece of steel plate.

The fun part is next. He paints the box with a hard, weather-proof enamel, making it a two-tone colour scheme: flame-red on top and speckled gunmetal blue on the lower half.

It dries while he has lunch.

Satisfied with his professional workmanship, Tong lovingly carries his new box out to the road in front of his house and places it next to the curb.

With pride, he looks down the road, seeing others parking their own, older, steel boxes.

Waving to an admiring neighbour, he retires to his house.

Later, Tong receives a call to go to a friend's house for a card game.

He jumps at the chance to show off his new steel box so he gets ready right away by putting on sunglasses and driving gloves.

Out at the curb, Tong picks up his steel box and carries it down the street, staying in the correct lane, properly waiting for traffic lights, all the while holding his box under his arm. At one of the red lights a young lady carrying a nice box nods at him and says, "New box?"

He smiles and nods proudly. "Yes. Just got the loan yesterday. It only took me a day to have it shining and ready, in front of my house!"

She is suitably impressed. "You have a big box!"

At his friend's house Tong finds a nearby parking spot, into which he parks his steel box. The parking meter demands five dollars per hour, which he pays by cellphone. Tong steps to his friend's house with a proud smile on his face.

· ·

Thanks for inspiration to:

Little Boxes, 1962, by Malvina Reynolds

sample:

> *And the boys go into business*
> *And marry and raise a family*
> *In boxes made of ticky tacky*
> *And they all look just the same.*
> *There's a green one and a pink one*
> *And a blue one and a yellow one,*
> *And they're all made out of ticky tacky*
> *And they all look just the same.*